PRAISE FOR WOJCIECH TOCHMAN

"Without judgment or commentary, [*Like Eating a Stone* . . .] lets the voices of the survivors relate this harrowing search. The result is a powerful portrayal of a country still suffering from the effects of war."
—*Financial Times*

"[Tochman's] style is all the more powerful for its restraint: outrage speaks terribly for itself, needs no hype, no color."
—*Sunday Times* (UK)

"[Tochman] relies on suggestive details on suggestive details, pungent quotes and simple, understated prose that is mannered at times but powerful in its own way."
—**Matthew Price,** (*The New York Times Book Review*)

ROOSTERS CROW, DOGS CRY

WOJCIECH TOCHMAN

Translated by Antonia Lloyd-Jones

OPEN LETTER
LITERARY TRANSLATIONS FROM THE UNIVERSITY OF ROCHESTER

Originally published in Polish as *Pianie Kogutów, Płacz Psów* by Wydawnictwo Literackie

Paperback: 978-1-948830-50-8 | Ebook: 978-1-948830-49-2

Library of Congress Cataloging-in-Publication Data: Available.

The quote on pg. 121 is from *Regarding the Pain of Others* by Susan Sontag, published by Picador Modern Classics (November 7, 2017).

This project is supported in part by an award from the National Endowment for the Arts and the New York State Council on the Arts with the support of the Governor of New York State and the New York State Legislature.

Cover design by Daniel Benneworth-Grey
Interior design by Anuj Mathur

Open Letter is the University of Rochester's nonprofit, literary translation press: Dewey Hall, 1-219, RC Box 278968, Rochester, NY 14627

www.openletterbooks.org

Printed on permanent/durable acid-free paper.

CONTENTS

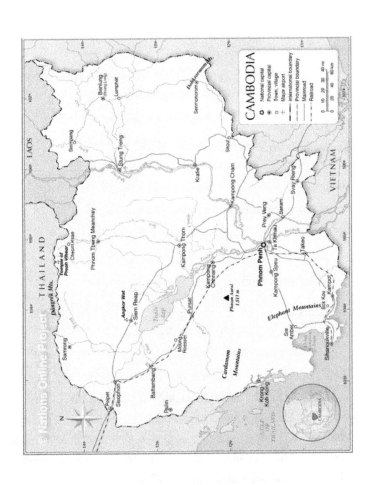

HISTORICAL TIMELINE

1863-1953
Cambodia is under French colonial rule.

1941
Prince Norodom Sihanouk becomes king.
Cambodia is occupied by Japan during World War II.

1946
France re-imposes its protectorate. A new constitution permits Cambodians to form political parties. Communist guerrillas begin an armed campaign against the French.

1953-1970 SIHANOUK ADMINISTRATION

1953
Cambodia wins its independence from France. Under King Sihanouk, it becomes the Kingdom of Cambodia.

1965
Sihanouk allows North Vietnamese guerrillas to set up bases

in Cambodia as part of their campaign against the US-backed government in South Vietnam.

1969

The US begins a secret bombing campaign against North Vietnamese forces on Cambodian soil.

1970-1975 KHMER REPUBLIC AND THE CIVIL WAR

1970

Prime Minister Lon Nol overthrows Sihanouk. He proclaims the Khmer Republic and sends the army to fight the North Vietnamese in Cambodia.

1975

Lon Nol is overthrown by the communist Khmer Rouge led by Pol Pot. Sihanouk briefly becomes head of state, the country is re-named Kampuchea.

All city dwellers are forcibly moved to the countryside to become agricultural workers. Money becomes worthless, basic freedoms are curtailed and religion is banned. The Khmer Rouge coin the phrase "Year Zero."

Hundreds of thousands of the educated middle-classes are tortured and executed in special centers. Others starve, or die from disease or exhaustion. The total death toll during the next three years is estimated to be at least 1.7 million.

1975-1979 KHMER ROUGE ERA

1976

The country is re-named Democratic Kampuchea. Sihanouk resigns, Khieu Samphan becomes head of state, Pol Pot is prime minister.

1977

Fighting breaks out with Vietnam.

1978

Vietnamese forces invade in a lightning assault.

1979-1993 VIETNAMESE OCCUPATION

1979

January – The Vietnamese take Phnom Penh. Pol Pot and Khmer Rouge forces flee to the border region with Thailand.

The People's Republic of Kampuchea is established. Many elements of life before the Khmer Rouge take-over are re-established.

1981

The pro-Vietnamese Kampuchean People's Revolutionary Party wins parliamentary elections. The international community refuses to recognize the new government. The government-in-exile, which includes the Khmer Rouge and Sihanouk, retains its seat at the United Nations.

1985

Cambodia is plagued by guerrilla warfare. Hundreds of thousands become refugees.

1989

Vietnamese troops withdraw. To attract foreign investment, socialism is abandoned, the country is re-named the State of Cambodia, and Buddhism is re-established as the state religion.

1991

A peace agreement is signed in Paris. A UN transitional authority shares power temporarily with representatives of the various factions in Cambodia. Sihanouk becomes head of state.

1993 TO PRESENT

1993

A general election sponsored by the UN leads to a coalition government. The monarchy is restored, Sihanouk becomes king again. The country is re-named the Kingdom of Cambodia.

1994

Thousands of Khmer Rouge guerrillas surrender in a government amnesty.

1997

Cambodian People's Party leader Hun Sen deposes his coalition partners. The Khmer Rouge put Pol Pot on trial and sentence him to life imprisonment.

1998

April – Pol Pot dies in his jungle hideout.

2001

A law setting up a tribunal to bring genocide charges against Khmer Rouge leaders is passed. International donors, encouraged by reform efforts, pledge $560 million in aid.

2003

The Cambodian People's Party (CPP), led by Hun Sen, wins general elections but fails to secure sufficient majority to govern alone, and in 2004 another coalition is formed.

2004

Parliament ratifies the kingdom's entry into the World Trade Organization (WTO). King Sihanouk abdicates and is succeeded by his son Norodom Sihamoni.

2007

UN-backed tribunals begin questioning Khmer Rouge suspects about allegations of genocide.

2010

The former Khmer Rouge leader known as Duch, who ran the notorious Tuol Sleng prison, is found guilty of crimes against humanity and given a thirty-five-year prison sentence.

2011
The three most senior surviving Khmer Rouge members, including Pol Pot's right-hand man, Nuon Chea, go on trial on charges of genocide and crimes against humanity.

2012
Cambodia and Thailand withdraw their troops from a disputed border area in line with a ruling by the International Court of Justice which aims to halt outbreaks of armed conflict in recent years.

2012
The former king, Norodom Sihanouk, dies of a heart attack at age eighty-nine.

2013
Former Khmer Rouge foreign minister Ieng Sary dies while awaiting trial for genocide. Following parliamentary elections, the CPP claims victory, but the opposition alleges widespread irregularities, and mass protests follow.

2014
The Cambodia National Rescue Party (CNRP)—the only significant opposition party—agrees to end its year-long boycott of parliament as part of an agreement with Hun Sen to break the deadlock over the disputed 2013 election.

A UN-backed court in Cambodia sentences two senior Khmer Rouge leaders, Nuon Chea and Khieu Samphan, to life in prison. They are the first top Khmer Rouge figures to be jailed. Further indictments of former Khmer Rouge commanders follow.

2015

January – Prime Minister Hun Sen marks thirty years in power.

2016

Prime Minister Hun Sen declares a political "ceasefire" following a wave of prosecutions of opposition members ahead of elections in 2018. The opposition CNRP resumes its parliamentary boycott over alleged threats from the ruling party. CNRP leader Sam Rainsy (in self-imposed exile since 2005) is sentenced to five years in prison after a document is published on his Facebook page, which the government says is a forgery. New legislation effectively bans him from taking part in politics.

2017

Sam Rainsy resigns as head of the CNRP and is replaced by human rights activist Kem Sokha, but Sokha is charged with treason, and the Supreme Court dissolves the CNRP.

OPERATION UNCHAIN

She's gazing high into the treetops; her business is with the birds, she's mimicking their warbling. One day she ran into the jungle, night fell, but she didn't come home, so her mother hired people to look for her. It wasn't easy—she must have gone a long way, or maybe she was scared and had hidden close to home, like a cat. What if she'd been eaten by wild animals? Or if spirits had taken her? Everything here has a spirit—the jungle, the stream, the precipice. Maybe she'd run into some evil people? Someone who cast spells? For five blazing days and five airless nights her family didn't know the answer. They thought she must have gotten lost, forgotten the way home. What if she'd forgotten her own name? Did she realize she wasn't alone when she went astray, and that she had to keep her unborn child safe, too? Or maybe she didn't want to save the child. Maybe she was hoping to lose it in the jungle. Hand it over to the nocturnal fiends that feed on fetuses? Some months ago she'd said she'd been taken by force. She'd put it curtly, in a single sentence. At that point she could still say what was troubling her, what was seething in her head. Though less and less precisely. So the family don't know the details of the incident that happened in the nearby town of Battambang. She went to live there with her mother after her parents' divorce.

Her father won't divulge the reasons for the marital split. Their three children went off with their mother, leaving him alone in the village. Here, where we're standing now. His daughter left in good health, she was gone for two years, but she came back in a different state. Her mind had shrunk as fast as her belly had grown.

She's thirty years old. Her son is now twelve. Every day the boy hears his mother chirping, trilling, and twittering. He can see how she's growing more distant all the time. A bird in a cage but without a bird's keen eye: hers are calm, fixed on something her hands can't reach. Eyes and hands that aren't interested in anything nearby. Or anyone. Thirteen years ago someone finally brought her home. All the way from the Thai border. Her body was naked, sore, and injured, though strong and healthy, ready to give birth. But her soul was absent.

And to this day her soul remains absent. Apart from that, she has a neat haircut, clean clothes, and a plump figure—she clearly gets enough rice. The cage? She's been there for several months; earlier, she sat in the old pigsty behind the house, chained by the foot. So she wouldn't run off into the jungle to look for her soul. So she wouldn't come back even more badly harmed by people. The pigsty is there as before, on the other side of the house, so we go look at it and take pictures: four pillars driven firmly into the ground, with a shoddy little roof on top that barely shields the patch of earth underneath. How many years did she spend on that dirt floor? It's hard to establish the facts. One time her father says three years, another time he says eleven. The calendar isn't his strong point. Like many people here, he lives outside time. Is he happy? More so now, perhaps. But when his prodigal daughter gave birth in her state of madness to a child of rape, he wasn't in the least bit happy. How could he be, when he felt nothing at all? After his wife abandoned him, he grew thin, stopped growing rice, and felt a pain in his chest, so he sold the cow, took the money to the pagoda, and asked the monks for salvation. Did they give him a miraculous cure for his distress? An elixir, perhaps? Some sacred amulets? Did they promise his mood would improve? In the next life, for sure. At the time, his chained-up daughter was being fed by her aunt. What about her mother? She never came. According to the father, she still hasn't come to this day. We could ask him who decided that. And we do. She never comes, we are told, no one knows why.

"I devoted myself to religion," says the father. "Every day I drank different herbs, and gradually I understood their miraculous powers, until the angel of God came to see me. It was like a dream, but I was awake. The angel explained to me which plants are for which illnesses, when to pick them, how to chop them up, how much to use, how long to boil them in water, leaves or roots, which to eat raw, which in the morning and which at night. He left when he was sure I had committed it all to memory. Now I heal people's stomachs, hearts, and livers. I can save people affected by black magic, I can break spells. My daughter? I poured water over her head for several hours to cleanse her body, while patiently imploring the spirits to leave her. I tried for many years, three, five, eleven. It was all in vain, for the spirits weren't living in my daughter at all. Finally, not long ago, some people came from a foreign organization, a union of Khmers in America and Canada. They were generous. They left a thousand dollars to build a cage. And they left without checking if we'd spent the money for that purpose. I don't remember which organization it was, I think it had the word 'humanity' in its name. I built the cage properly, I spent every last cent of the donated money on it. It's nice, as you can see, it's solid, hygienic, and comfortable."

Aluminum bars sunk upright into concrete, at regular intervals a few inches apart, each ten feet high, form the four walls of the cage. A square, ten feet by ten feet, topped with a tin roof. A padlocked door. The floor is paved with bright terracotta tiles, easy to clean. Down the center there's a sloping channel to flush away waste matter. It's surrounded by dense greenery, deep shadows, and a chorus of birds. When the sun is up. Because when it sets, it's so quiet and so dark around here that it's hard to believe the light will ever return. This will be her home when she gets better too—her father still believes the day will come, or maybe that's just the impression he wants to give. "I'll remove the padlock and the door will open forever."

"A daughter's home is her father's house," says Dr. Ang Sody in a chilly tone, looking at the large yellow building standing nearby. She signals to the driver: end of visit. We move on. We'll be back to see Talan again. That's the name of the woman in the cage. Schizophrenia—that's the name of her illness, according to Dr. Sody.

His name is Kim. Twenty-seven years old. Thin, naked, smiling. He lives in a large, bright room. Three barred windows look out in three directions. Between one set of bars and another there's a hammock. Under the hammock there's white terracotta tiling. In the adjoining space there's a toilet. The door to the outside is always locked from the outside. There are no bad smells, it's clean—evidently, his aunt takes care of her nephew. She's not much older than he is, only about ten or fifteen years. "Put something on," she tells him as we come up to say hello.

The walled cell stands in the village of O Ta Poung, in Pursat province, right beside National Highway 5. All day and night, rain or shine, the cars race along here from Phnom Penh to Battambang. Or in the opposite direction. The asphalt pavement is narrow and potholed, there's a lot of traffic, and the drivers sound their horns and speed by with no regard for others. The noise from the road doesn't seem to bother Kim. Though he clearly does take notice of his surroundings. He looks in our direction trustingly, amicably, and sticks his thin hands through the bars, wanting us to come and stand near him. What will we learn from him today? Nothing. He doesn't say a word.

The medical diagnosis for him is psychosis.

There's an improvement—his aunt doesn't try to hide her satisfaction. And she tells us his parents died thirteen years ago. In a single year: first his father, then his mother. AIDS. He had a sister. She went away. Where did she go? What's she doing? No idea. Kim, an orphan, has been left with no one but his aunt. And his grandmother, who's staring at us as if we weren't here at all. Can she see the world in front of her nose? Or can she only see "all that," her past life? Everyone here remembers "all that," it's impossible to get it out of your mind. The grandmother doesn't say a word. She just chain-smokes cigarettes. Kim used to smoke too. Or rather, he used to heat up crystals that look like sugar and inhale the fumes. He'd go a long way from home, beat people up, and destroy their property. Until finally, about ten years ago, he flew off somewhere and failed to find his way back. That happens when you're addicted to methamphetamines, which in Cambodia are cheaply and widely available. He never had to go far to get them. The magical crystals were sold right here, in the village, around the clock. Kim has been sitting in his cell for five years. Dr. Ang Sody has been visiting him for the past three months.

"I don't know what to do," says Dr. Sody, looking at the naked man. The piece of furniture the man is lying on is called a kre. It's a knee-high wooden platform, around six feet by six feet square, sometimes shorter, sometimes wider, and we see them in every home. The kre serves as a bed, a table, or a bench. Family life takes place on and around it. Right here on the brown earth, on the dirt floor, underneath the house, because in Cambodia the houses are often built on tall pillars. There's usually a benevolent spirit living in one of the pillars, a guardian who protects the home from evil spirits. Sometimes we might see a kre outside the door, if the building stands flat on the ground. Then the kre is sheltered by some sort of awning, made of bamboo, coconut, tin, plastic, or whatever. The sun blazes. The rain pours, sometimes so heavily that you can't see a thing, not the sky, or the road, or the people on the road. The kre is always waiting for you, regardless of the weather. You can perch on the edge of it and chat to someone who has come to sit with you—your mother, or a neighbor—you can chop vegetables for soup, or cut up a chicken, you can eat your rice, do your lessons, or lie down comfortably and close your eyes when others aren't looking.

But the whole village is looking at the naked man. He's not moving. We're half a mile away from National Highway 6, which runs north from the capital to Siem Reap. The naked man's kre is under a large tamarind tree, at a point where the red road intersects another red road—outside a house, opposite a store. In this settlement, life goes on around the naked man's kre. But not family life. He has no family. He has no one to talk to. That's why

Dr. Sody doesn't know what to do. Now and then she makes the 125-mile journey here from Phnom Penh, half a day's drive, and does her best to help, but today she's met with disappointment.

My photographer and I have joined the Transcultural Psychosocial Organization's (TPO) traveling team. The TPO is a non-governmental organization of medics who work outside the Cambodian state health-care service to bring help, free of charge, to the mentally ill. Ang Sody is the first female psychiatrist in the country's history. Working alongside her is Seang Leap, a middle-aged male psychologist.

The naked man's name is Nel. He's forty, and he's been sick for half his life. According to Dr. Sody's diagnosis, it's schizophrenia. He's been on a chain for twenty years. Recently he'd been feeling better, because for three years he dutifully took his medicine, from the first time the doctor came here. To begin with, his sister would hide the pills in balls of rice, but then he started swallowing them with water without any help. She set her brother free, and five months ago she left for Thailand. To earn a living. With her husband and children. Their elderly father remained on the other side of the village, and there's medicine for his son at his place. In Cambodia they say it's better if your father dies than your mother. Better for your boat to sink than for your house to burn down. You only have a few small items in your boat, but you have everything in your house. A house will always give you shelter. Nel's mother died long ago, and his father never comes by. Dr. Sody can't see the point of talking to the father.

And Nel doesn't talk to anyone, he doesn't say anything, his eyes are open but he doesn't look at anyone, and he doesn't get dressed. He lies motionless all day and night. As if he weren't here. But sometimes he gets up, pours a pot of water over his head, and lies down again. He eats what the neighbors bring him. How many times a day? Not every day. Only when the sight of his hunger starts to prick the neighbors' conscience. So say the people in the shabby store opposite. We ask what they know about Nel, what they think about him lying there with no one to care for him. They reply in short phrases that don't add much: is it an illness, or black magic? No idea. No one has ever seen magic, have they? Maybe there are spirits living inside him—they clearly like it in there, it must be cozy, because they never leave him for an instant. They're not threatening anyone. Nobody in the village is afraid of Nel.

Without smiling, the psychiatrist listens to the people in the store. And makes a decision: she's not going to entrust their sick neighbor's medical care to them.

We drive away.

We don't go far.

To the nearest small town, which is called Kampong Kdei. Mrs. Sun lives here. Her husband's tall, walled house stands by National Highway 6, set back from the road behind a metal gate, in the depths of a lush garden. Behind the house, among some thick bushes, is Mrs. Sun's shed. It's a dark wooden box thatched with straw, about six feet by ten, less than two feet off the ground, on posts. A woman, aged sixty-five, locked up for almost forty years—that was the information sent by one of our interpreters, whose daily job is as a guide to the Angkor temples. We had asked him to inquire among his friends and neighbors about people who were confined. We're always asking people here if they know of anyone who's mentally ill. The interpreter has given us several phone numbers, including that of Mrs. Sun's husband.

Dr. Sody wants to see the new patient. She asks the husband to bring her out of the shed. The old man loosens the staple. In the doorway stands a thin woman with a shaved head. No speech, no facial expression, no interest in anything. She's frightened, but clean and dressed. The husband was expecting our visit. But he tells us that she usually spends her life naked and dirty. She tears at her clothes, shouts and cries day and night, then sometimes spends weeks in total silence. She eats every morning and evening, but can't control her bodily functions. Her husband has installed a pipe underneath the shed, and via an external ladder he only has to turn on a hydrant and there's a cold-water supply. Twice a week he rinses her body with a hose. Unless it's colder, as in January, when he does it once every two weeks. He cleans the wooden floor with a powerful jet of water. He bought a German-made compressor for the purpose.

"I met my wife on our wedding day," he replies in answer to our question about how it all started. "I'd seen photos of her in advance. Our parents knew each other, and came up with the idea that we should marry. I trusted their decision. It was 1972. I was twenty-two, and she was two years younger. A pretty face, a nice body. Clever. She'd graduated from high school. I'd failed the final exams. How did she feel? What did she think? I don't know. I never asked her about her feelings. She gave birth to our first daughter. We worked. We had a little general store. Then I traded door-to-door as well, on a bicycle. We could get half the store on that bicycle, you know. Sometimes I'd be away for three nights and four days. It was hard to travel around when the country was so unsettled. In those days, part of it belonged to General Lon Nol, who had deposed King Sihanouk and was still in charge of Phnom Penh, and part already belonged to Pol Pot. The war began. At that point I hadn't yet heard that Pol Pot was killing people. Villages were on fire from American air raids. There were bombs falling on our heads, with Phnom Penh's permission. Did we know that then? Did we understand it? I can't remember. We had to go on living. I would buy clothes, imported fabric and kramas—you know, Khmer scarves—in Svay Rieng province. I'd come back and sell them here. Also shrimp and lard. Until one day Pol Pot's people started to get dangerous. Night-time arrests, disappearances. That's how I lost two of my brothers. My wife and I pretended we couldn't read. But because of the store they saw us as capitalists anyway. They sent us into the jungle to cut down trees. We had nowhere to sleep. We built shacks to live in. Then they sent us to work in the rice fields. Then to build a dam. My wife gave birth to our second child, and then a third. She had difficult births, but there were no doctors. Someone noticed that she had started behaving oddly, talking to herself. I thought she was talking to the children. She had to grind rice and do the cleaning with a child at her dry breast from dawn to dusk. Then the Vietnamese came. We returned here, to Kampong Kdei. We found out who was still alive, who had died of starvation, and who'd been killed. My wife? Pregnant. She went out to get something. When she came back, she wasn't the same. On the way she'd seen an open grave: seventy-five bodies. Throats cut with thorny palm leaves.

"She gave birth to our fourth child in a state of insanity.

"We needed a kru immediately. A man who communicates with the spirits."

In Sanskrit, as we know from our research, a kru is a guru—a teacher or master. There are various kinds of kru. Here what was needed was a kru khmer—a healer. There are various different healers in Cambodia. Herbalists, folk healers, shamans, whisperers, and exorcists. Our interpreter throws them all in a single bag. He calls them traditional doctors.

The first traditional doctor prescribed herbs.

The second was absolutely sure: the hungry spirits of the victims in the mass grave had inhabited her body. For several days he beat the sick woman all over her body with a stick to drive them out. She asked why he was trying to kill her.

The third confirmed what the second had said. Hungry spirits. He doused her in boiling water. She was scalded.

The fourth, a Muslim, placed raw egg on the patient's toes. She screamed that her feet were burning. According to the husband, the eggs hardened. The healer said this was proof of the presence of an evil angel in Mrs. Sun's body.

"Where are you from?" asked the exorcist.

"From home," she replied.

They came back from the folk healer. She ran about the neighborhood naked. Something had to be done about it. It's been almost forty years since Mrs. Sun's husband locked her up. And that's how things have remained.

As the doctor listens to the husband's story she observes the patient; for some time she doesn't take her eyes off her, as if trying to inhabit her body like a good angel. To feel what Mrs. Sun is feeling. To see things as she sees them. There are some patent symptoms: she only talks to herself, incoherently, she takes her clothes off, she doesn't sleep at night, she doesn't recognize her family, and she doesn't know what's going on around her. Dr. Sody writes down the number of the illness: F29, which in the international classification means non-specific inorganic psychosis. The doctor asks the husband if he agrees to his wife's treatment. If so, please sign the documents, says Seang Leap, the psychologist. On a small metal tray the doctor uses a teaspoon to count out tablets, and tips them into sealed plastic bags the size of a packet of facial tissues. First, as ever, enough for thirty days. At the next visit they're usually prescribed enough for ninety. On each little bag there's a symbol: a half sun means morning, a whole sun means noon, a moon means evening. Under each symbol there's a little window where the doctor writes with marker: 0, ½, or 1. That explains how many tablets to give the patient in the morning, how many at noon, and how many in the evening.

"You are responsible for giving them to your wife," the psychologist tells the old man.

"Of course," says the husband, listening to it all carefully; from the start of our visit he's had his head bowed and an uneasy look on his face.

"The packets of medicine must be kept away from children," the psychologist warns, "and even more importantly, from the patient."

"Of course," agrees the old man, "of course."

Does he want us to go now? The situation evidently embarrasses him. He's not stupid. Who's ever seen a husband keeping his wife locked up? "I'm no exception," he says in parting. "Did you know that out in the countryside there are husbands in cages as well as wives?"

No, we didn't know that.

Mr. Tuol Sleng—that's what we dub him minutes after meeting him. There's a heavy shackle on his left calf. "That's the sort of shackle Pol Pot's men used to chain the prisoners at Tuol Sleng," says Leap, the psychologist.

The man's name is Hap. He's sitting on a narrow board under an awning made of dried palm leaves. He can move a couple of feet to the left and back again, because the shackle runs along a short metal rod. It's the sort of bar that's used on construction sites to reinforce concrete.

He resembles a hippie who's been through the wringer: a faraway look in his eyes, a thin body, long hair, a long beard, a rag around his hips. Fifty-five years old. For the past twenty, ever since his wife locked him up in here, he hasn't been able to stand or even raise himself up a bit. The roof is too low.

But his vacant eyes do notice us, though they're tired and resigned, and there's not a spark to be seen in them. We don't talk. There's no contact.

Palm trees as tall as towers grow in a straight row. Next to them there's a haystack. And a cow. Cow pies all around. And plastic bags into which the sick man defecates. That much he can do. And he can eat with his hands. Twice a day he's given a little rice in a bowl. He doesn't wash or shave. Sometimes, when the rain lashes down, it spatters him under the awning.

Closer to the highway there's a small, windowless straw house standing on three-foot-high posts. There's a housewife bustling around inside it. A small woman with white hair, in brightly colored clothes, eyes fixed on the ground, a quiet voice. A demon has taken up residence in her husband, that's plain to see, because more than once or twice it has defended itself by driving someone away, or trying to hit them. Leave me alone, he'd shout, don't kill me! There'd be no one near him. Just the neighbors watching from afar. And they did want to kill. At home, Hap used to beat his wife and children. In the countryside that's not unusual. But he was attacking people at random on the road as well. He had a lot of strength, so people kept a wary eye on him. Until one day he went too far. He set fire to the neighbors' wooden cabin. Immediately, the axes were at the ready—in Cambodia, mob law is common practice. There was very nearly a lynching, or a beheading, but his wife came to his defense.

They'd married some time ago, not at their parents' bidding, but out of love, which isn't common in the Khmer countryside, so how could she let her husband come to such an end? She bargained with the neighbors, promising to tie him up, and that he wouldn't do any more harm; she guaranteed he wouldn't accost anyone or go anywhere. Then some soldiers had been summoned to help her imprison her husband.

Did he shout when he was shackled to the metal rod? By day or at night?

"He did," says his wife, waving a hand. "Until he stopped. He's mute."

Various questions occur to us during the journey: Why are the sick people silent? Have they lost their voices? Their language? Is it a result of their illness? Or all those years in captivity? Which symptoms result from the first, and which from the second? Does every noncommunicative patient sink so deep into the world of their own morbid sensations, or is it just their way of surviving? Can total and utter withdrawal have its origin in the trauma of captivity, rather than in illness? Have things ever been different? Has anyone been chained because of their evil nature, or aggression brought on by alcohol, and only sunk into true madness after being locked up?

We never get a precise answer. Neither from the families or the doctor. Evidently, Dr. Sody herself can't find that out from the relatives. Or perhaps she doesn't have the time to identify the individual symptoms? Because she has to get going now, she has to move on, to go and see the next imprisoned person. The chain is never a cure—that's how she responds to our doubts. "The chain always drags them over the edge."

Mr. Tuol Sleng used to be a soldier. He was wounded in the back, and it took him ages to recover; it's ancient history. This is his property. The fields are negligible, the grass is covered in shit. They used to own more, a large house nearby made of wood, but on concrete supports. They sold almost everything for treatment with expensive healers. What about a medical doctor? Yes, his wife had once been to the health center five hundred yards from here, on the highway, on her own, because her husband was sitting on his board, he'd been shackled for several years by then. The doctor hadn't seen the patient, hadn't even expressed the need—he'd simply accepted his fee and given her a six-month supply of tablets. They'd cost a lot of money, but they hadn't helped at all. The wife never went back for more. "I did everything I could to get my husband cured," she says today. "Until finally the love was all gone. Only pity remained. But I have no choice. I won't harm him—that has never crossed my mind for an instant. He's still my husband. A human being. Any harm I do to another person will always come back to me. Or to someone else in the family. I hope he dies soon, that would be the best for him."

Everyone would then breathe a sigh of relief. Both the wife, and the eldest son, who is thirty, but still doesn't have a family. He can't have one, because he's caring for his father. And he'll continue to do so if his mother passes away first. She often says she's had enough of life. If he got married now, he'd have to take care of his wife and children. He'd have to forget about his parents, at least in the financial sense—such are the local customs.

There may be another reason why the son is single, Dr. Sody tells us. Mental illness—or what many people here believe to be a possession by spirits—is a stigma for the entire family. A chain or a cage is like a brand that bears witness: here they give birth to lunatics. This house is no good. Our daughters must avoid him.

Will the wife and son release Mr. Hap when he gets better? For now Dr. Sody diagnoses alcohol-induced psychosis. She counts out the tablets and explains to the woman how to give them to her husband. He should get better.

"I'll never let him out," says the wife, "or he'll go drink with the neighbors again. They all drink here. They won't leave him alone."

They drink everywhere.

In the southeast too, on the other side of the country, closer to the Vietnamese border. Here, in the village of Knor Khang Tboung, on a farm amid the rice fields lives a man who's been set free. His name is Chan-moeun. He completed high school. He used to be a boxer. He was a husband and father before forty. An alcoholic. His wife took their child and ran away to the city, where she works; once a month she comes to see her husband for an hour, and brings him a small sum of money. "He drank so much alcohol that it drove him mad," says Chan-moeun's mother. "He never slept. He started talking nonsense. Shouting. Smashing things. He'd hit me for no reason. I couldn't allow that. He ended up on a chain."

"Psychosis," confirmed Dr. Sody the first time she came here. Chan-moeun was given medicine. And a warning: if combined with alcohol, the tablets can kill you. Taken regularly they can help. And some months later, his reason returned. Then his mother gave an ultimatum: "I'll let you out, but if you get drunk just one more time, I'll chain you up for good."

What does he do all day? He hasn't recovered enough strength to work, and he's unable to concentrate. He sits, or walks around the green fields. The village drinkers, his old pals and some new ones too, try to persuade him to join them. He tells them he can't, because of the medicine. They refuse to believe it, they laugh and mock him. Then he raises his pant leg. He always goes around in long pants, which is very rare for men in the countryside. He shows his pals the metal ring clamped above his ankle, still padlocked by his mother. It's a weapon against the drinkers, effective so far. Like an initiation ring. On his walks, the boxer visits an imprisoned woman who lives in the neighboring village. The one who killed her own father.

Two sisters are saving up for their father's mourning ceremony. The third sister killed him. The first ceremony has to take place seven days after death. They've already held that one. But the second ceremony, one hundred days later, has to be grander. If they fail to organize it, evil spirits will remain in the village. And the entire village believes that's what will happen. It's been a month since the one hundredth day; the sisters are neglecting the customs, and the neighbors' anxiety is rising. Because the soul of the murdered man is refusing to leave, it's wandering around their homesteads, roaming the rice fields, growing more enraged, prowling along the paths, along the canals and the weirs. It needs help. But inviting the entire village costs a fortune: you must set up a large tent, hire tables and chairs, provide food, drink, music, and an offering for the monks for their holy rituals—that's at least five hundred dollars, usually more. The more generous the

payment at the pagoda, the greater the chance for the spirit of
the murdered father to have an onward journey. And the more
hope for his return in a better life and time.

Along with riels, dollars are in daily use in Cambodia. Most
often one-dollar bills, because with those you can buy soup at
the bazaar, or rice with carrots or some leaves. The sisters are
seamstresses. They spend two dollars a day on food. They earn
two hundred a month. They work at a factory six days a week,
from 7 A.M. to 4 P.M., with an hour's break for lunch. They make
famous brand-name jeans. The Chinese owner exports the
goods to the Japanese and European markets. The two sisters
live and work in Phnom Penh, in a district far from downtown
that smells of burning plastic. But where in Phnom Penh can't
you smell something? Trash cans stewing in the heat, urine,
sewers, burning dog hair, burning flesh, melted fat, meat.

The first sister pays thirty dollars a month to rent a room.
The second rents one half the size three streets away. She's lived
here for twenty years, so she gets a discount. The rooms? Holes
in a wooden barrack, three paces by two, enough space for a bed,
and a nail on which to hang your clothes or a fly swatter. By the
bed there's a shelf for a pot and a bowl. And that's it. Outside the
door there are some large vats of water. The owner of the site fills
them for a small fee. Here the working women wash, and here
they cook rice on a black kitchen range. There are toilets behind
the barrack. In front of it is the owner's two-story stone house.
There are other seamstresses living in the barrack, behind thin
walls that don't extend to the ceiling. One seamstress in each
partition, sometimes three. Usually single, not married, married
but abandoned, or having abandoned, divorced, or widowed—it
varies. They've left their children somewhere in the countryside,

with their grandparents or aunts, or else they've lost them, like the younger of the two sisters.

The younger one's name is Phally, she's thirty-three, and has a son she hasn't seen for nine years. He had just started to walk when he and her husband disappeared. Turns out her mother-in-law had decided her son shouldn't be involved with a seamstress and deserved a better woman. Phally traveled to her house, several times, and begged for her child back, but her mother-in-law was unmoved by her lament. And there was no trace of her son. Should Phally have gone to the police? It never occurred to her—her husband has money, and the police like the stuff. A poor person who clashes with a rich one has no chance here. Too bad! Nothing else had happened. No more information. Phally has no money; all she does is look at her phone every day, at a photograph of her son from nine years ago. And every day she weeps when no one's looking. In Cambodia, nobody shows their tears in public.

The other sister, Savin, aged thirty-seven, also has a child far away. Her teenage daughter lives in a province near the Vietnamese border, at the home of her uncle—the three sisters' brother. Their brother's not interested in any of it, he doesn't care about the mourning ceremonies, nor does he contribute to the family expenses; he has no money, he just grows rice. Savin's daughter is doing fine at her uncle's place. Savin only has one thing to say about her husband—they're separated, and we don't ask her further questions. We're interested in Sinuon, the third, youngest sister, who lives eighty miles away from Phnom Penh, also close to the Vietnamese border, in a village, outside her parents' house. Chained up. It's her we're supposed to be talking about today, not her sisters.

We went to see Sinuon a few days ago. Everyone there wishes she were dead.

"What about us? We wish her good health," declare her two sisters, looking at each other in disbelief. They can't quite believe what they're saying. She looked all right when they had a party at the village to celebrate the last Khmer New Year. She was smiling, chatty, everything was fine. She was very attentive to her infant son.

But affectionate? Sometimes we think nobody understands that sort of question here, as if affection is a tricky concept. Sinuon has been through a lot. Her husband chased other women, she was mad with jealousy, and she left the village for Phnom Penh to punish him for his affairs. He wasn't upset by her absence and petitioned for divorce. That was the start of her illness—according to the doctors at the Khmer-Soviet Friendship Hospital. That's the name of a clinic in the capital where the psychiatrists work. After the divorce, Sinuon lost her mind—or so the doctors said, according to her sisters, because she was devoting too much thought to her husband. Poor girl, say the sisters, imagine going crazy over a guy. Or perhaps something else triggered an illness that was dormant within her. After arriving in the capital, Sinuon worked at a restaurant. Something must have happened to her there. Maybe it wasn't an ordinary restaurant, but some other kind—the sisters are having trouble with their words. Anyway, one night when she was at work, someone hit her on the head. A well-informed friend told the sisters about it. Did Sinuon take drugs? The sisters look now at us, now at each other—the kind friend never said a word about that. Except that once things were bad, Sinuon returned home to the village. Their parents

were both still alive then. Soon after, their mother died, maybe
out of fear of her daughter's illness.

Was she dangerous, or aggressive? Not at first, but later on
she went running down the road with a knife, so their father
caught her, chained her up by one arm and a leg, and secured her
to one of the twelve pillars supporting his grand house. One time
a policeman looked in on her. Her arm was bleeding because of
the chain—he frowned and shook his head. "Just leave the chain
on her leg, she's not going to run away."

One day, after a year in captivity, a doctor came from Phnom
Penh to see Sinuon. There was a psychologist with her. Someone
had written to them on Facebook about the chained woman.
They had talked to the father, and perhaps they had managed
to exchange a word with the patient too, but probably not. Dr.
Sody had confirmed Sinuon's diagnosis of psychosis. It may have
been prompted by drugs, or perhaps something else, the doctor
wasn't sure. She prescribed some tablets. After three months'
treatment, the father released his daughter—she had calmed
down, she was talking, she could work. She cleaned trash from
the street in a nearby town, bits of plastic, or cabbage leaves at
the market, and in the afternoon she came home. Until one day
she stabbed her father eighteen times with a knife.

Dr. Ang? No one ever calls her that, although Ang is her family
name. Sody Ang? Not that either, because here the family name
comes before the first name. She's usually called by her first
name, Dr. Sody. She's always in pants ironed with a crease, and a
shirt with a collar, usually of a pale color. She has gray hair tied
in a short ponytail. Her smile is rare. Her step is sure.

Like her male and female colleagues at the Transcultural Psychosocial Organization, Dr. Sody receives patients at a clinic in a district on the edge of Phnom Penh. Here the specialists run support groups and psycho-education. Commissioned by a tribunal appointed to judge the crimes of the Khmer Rouge, they support survivors who have to make statements in the presence of their torturers. "All that" has affected every Khmer family and cannot be forgotten. But, says Dr. Sody, we can't only seek the reasons for people's current anguish in all that.

In a nutshell: poverty drives people mad.

In Cambodia, as we read on the TPO website, there's a huge gulf between what's needed and what's available. There should be a psychiatrist working at every health center. But there are only fifty psychiatrists in the entire country, and over sixteen million people. Almost all the psychiatrists work at hospitals in the capital. And the capital is the only place where there are psychiatric wards. Two of them. Fewer than twenty beds for the entire country. Usually they're not occupied, because people can't afford the hospital, or consultations at private clinics. There are several in Phnom Penh, for the rich.

That's why the TPO specialists travel around the country. They do their best to reach those whose poor and helpless families have chained them behind houses, in banana groves, cells, pigsties, cubicles, and cages. Their sole patients are people who've been locked up because of mental illness.

That means they don't visit the majority of mentally sick people.

Most of the people who suffer from various mental disorders are not aggressive, as every psychiatrist will confirm; these patients do no harm and aren't a threat to anyone, nor do they destroy anything. At most they give their neighbors cause for some stupid jokes, for laughter and mockery—if they ever come out of their houses. Many never do. They hide from the world out of fear. It is their illness, not their relatives, that imprisons them. The traveling psychiatric team has no time for them. They'll be given help if they can get to the TPO clinic in Phnom Penh.

The patients sentenced to house arrest by their own families are those who have attacked someone, repeatedly destroyed things, or robbed their neighbors. Fear of aggression is the reason for their imprisonment, but not the only one. There's another one that concerns the women—and not necessarily the dangerous ones. Their families are afraid they won't be able to keep an eye on a sick female relative: she might wander too far from home and be raped. A scenario that's quite likely—so say the doctor and the psychologist, as well as the sick women's relatives. Some of the families don't seem to think rape is as dreadful as its possible consequences. A child born of a lunatic as the result of rape will grow up with a stigma that can never be erased. So to avoid a child who's branded, it's better to shut the sick woman in a cage, chain her up, or lock her inside.

Operation Unchain—that's what the TPO staff call their work in the field.

Usually they drive north from Phnom Penh along National Highway 6, the length of Lake Tonlé Sap on its eastern side, all the way to the city of Siem Reap, familiar to tourists because of the nearby Angkor temples. Then they go northwest, then make a sharp turn down the map toward the Thai border, and take National Highway 5 along the western shore of the lake, back to Phnom Penh. That's over six hundred miles, a week at cheap hotels with cheap food. Once an hour, or once every two hours, they make a stop. Not near the highway, but usually somewhere off to the left down a red gravel road, or to the right, into the bushes or the rice fields, to a sick man's home. But more often a sick woman's. According to the TPO staff, it's usually women who suffer from mental disorders in Cambodia.

What does Dr. Sody tell us about herself in the car? Nothing. When she's not on the road, she receives patients at the TPO clinic in the mornings. Her office is just past the reception desk, on the right. There's a line of patients waiting outside, most of them women. The most common diagnosis is depression. Behind the depression lies poverty. Behind the poverty there's illiteracy, unemployment, slave labor, child labor, people-trafficking, prostitution, corruption, abused wives, abused children, rape, alcohol, and methamphetamines. People borrow money from a sort of shadow banking system, they don't have any money for the next loan repayment, they lose their houses, and go crazy. They can also lose their homes without falling into debt—the rich evict the poor when they need their land back to build tower blocks and factories. The police, the army, and the bulldozers are paid, and the family heads into homelessness. Sometimes poverty forces people to live in the jungle. But they're cutting down the jungle too—in Cambodia, deforestation is happening on an unprecedented scale. The homeless have nowhere to go. They build shacks on the edge of the highway. They're not sure if they'll be run over, or if they'll have anything to eat tomorrow. There's no pleasure in life. No relaxation, no let-up. Khmer wives rarely leave their husbands. But the husbands disappear; they commit suicide. Or they don't. Either way they both sink to the bottom. That, put very briefly, is what Dr. Sody tells us about her everyday patients. At the clinic she tries to bolster them. She talks to them and prescribes antidepressants.

Sometimes a family comes to the TPO clinic with a person literally in chains. They're usually patients from the neighborhood, from Phnom Penh. The TPO doesn't go visit chained patients who live nearby. Even local poor people can get to the clinic. But do they all come? Not all. The patients often live somewhere in the city center, in the back streets, in gloomy courtyards or damp hovels, hidden away from the public eye. Their families are afraid to show them to the world. Why should strangers have to know that one of their relatives is suffering from a mental illness? Or is possessed by spirits, because even in the big city people believe in spirits. No one wants to marry into a family like that, says Dr. Sody, repeating what she's already told us. The sick person's brothers and sisters have a hard time finding partners.

Will Dr. Sody tell us a bit about herself? Maybe another time.

Now we're all standing in a banana grove—the doctor, the psychologist, the driver, my photographer, my interpreter, and I—behind a shabby, empty house at the very center of a village named Prey, less than two miles from the highway. Opposite the house, on the other side of a concrete road, there's a wooden police station. Next to that is the wooden office of a British NGO that explains to the citizens on posters that they should wash their hands. And they must defecate in the latrines, not just anywhere. This is our first time here. The sun is blazing, some large leaves provide a good deal of shade, but not much relief. We're looking at a young man. The neighbors are looking too, as if they'd never seen him before, but they know him well. They've come running from the fields and from their houses; curious about our visit, they've dropped their work or their afternoon rest. There are some children too. They're all laughing. But the adults are talking about their fears: what if the chain breaks one day?

The man's name is Rean. He's shackled to one of the four concrete pillars supporting a square roof. He lives under this structure, ten feet by ten feet. For about three years now, apparently. He's tall, thin, dirty, and naked. He squats. He stands up. He casts us a hostile glare. He mutters. He scratches his head, his body. He paces. Agitated, tense, angry. Five feet this way, five feet back. The doctor asks him his name. There's no answer. How old are you? Silence. A nasty look. Rage. He squats again. Stands up. And suddenly picks up a stick. Writes something with it on the dirt. The psychologist tries to decipher the signs. The doctor tries too. They can't make heads or tails of it. The world of insanity is closed to the sound-of-mind, quite literally. Even to those who by reason of their profession are doing their best to understand the illness. It's no good. There's no way in. There's no contact with the prisoner. Now the man is lying in a dirty hammock stretched between the pillars. He doesn't take his eyes off us for a moment. There's no respite. His aunt puts on a face mask, her expression is firm and displeased, she studiedly ignores us, picks up a plastic bottle, and walks toward the sick man from behind; he hasn't noticed her yet, she has a few seconds to spare, she's watching closely in case he makes an abrupt movement. Then she quickly douses the ground around the hammock and walks off beyond the reach of the chain. A couple of pints of water are supposed to kill that odor? From a safe distance the aunt throws a second bottle in her nephew's direction. It's filled with drinking water. Half a pint. After the bottle comes a plastic bag containing boiled rice, which lands under the hammock. The portion in the bag would fit on a medium-sized plate. That's all Rean is given to eat and drink. Twice a day. There are hundreds of plastic bags lying around. Each one contains the sick man's feces.

We walk to the other side of the road, to the police station. We sit at a table; there are some documents on it, no one's in charge of them, there's no one here; the air is still, the policemen have gone off somewhere. And the guys next door, from the British outfit, haven't come to work today. Dr. Sody works regardless of the weather. She talks to the sick man's aunt. From behind the shabby house we can hear him shouting. "He roars like that for days and nights on end," says the aunt. "Like a wounded beast. He used to be calm, polite, sociable, he helped people, he went to high school, he was learning English, he had plans to go abroad. And look how far he's gone. To a chain. To public ridicule. To my torment. Why have you come here? I don't want him to be saved. The doctors from Siem Reap have already treated him. After their tablets he ate so much that it was impossible to keep up. I took him off the medicine."

Dr. Sody shakes her head, she doesn't say much, one sentence, two at most: "He's a human being. Your sister gave birth to him."

"He killed my sister," replies the aunt. "He killed his own mother and father."

The aunt's story, in short: his parents? Neither poor, nor well-off. They had family in the United States. The father's relatives knew some Khmers with American citizenship, who were refugees in Pol Pot's day; they'd managed to escape to Thailand, and then to the United States. They had a pretty daughter, born over there, and they were looking for a husband for her in the homeland. No one was surprised by that—arranged marriages are still common among the Khmers. And since Rean looked like Antonio Banderas, with a broad smile, a seductive stare, a sense of humor, and thick black hair, they thought perhaps he should be introduced to the Khmer American girl. Everyone wants to get out of here, let him at least succeed.

The families agreed that even if they didn't love each other, the marriage would happen—let the boy leave the village far from the highway, let him get set up in America. In time his wife would come to love him, and they'd have children.

Rean's parents paid for his fiancée's journey. She flew to Siem Reap after changing planes in Singapore. They traveled around the country together, visited Phnom Penh, and saw the sea in Sihanoukville. And according to the aunt, Rean fell in love. What was her name? The aunt can't remember. And she doesn't know if the refugees' daughter reciprocated Rean's love. She left, he started learning English, he was planning to go after her. She came back. They got married according to their parents' plan. The aunt calls it a fake or paper marriage. Does that mean the marriage wasn't legitimate? The aunt is inconsistent in her account—she isn't sure. But she repeats that the wedding wasn't real, but a sham. They had to lie to the local authorities, in order to get a valid marriage certificate. The certificate was issued. The fake wife, as the aunt insists on calling her, had to go back to America again, and her family paid for him to go on studying English. They didn't see each other for two years. Why? The aunt doesn't know. Then the illness came. The polite Rean vanished, and the dangerous, nasty, aggressive one appeared. He destroyed things and beat up his parents. It was impossible to talk sense into him. This went on for some time. The father fell ill because of the beatings, possibly because of alcohol—he was drinking more and more, and his wife was drinking with him. They both had weak livers and weak hearts, they both lost strength, they weren't able to defend themselves against their son. One day Rean took up a piece of wood and hit his father on the head. And that was the end of the father. He grabbed his mother by the hand, and spun her body in the air, again and again as if throwing a lasso. And he struck his mother against the ground. She died because of that, out of fear, or maybe because of a ruined liver, about a year after the father.

Rean has three brothers, all of whom live in Thailand. They came to the mother's funeral and went away again. The police came to see the aunt, as did the neighbors. "We have children here," they said. The police gave orders for Rean to be imprisoned. "So I imprisoned him," the aunt tells Dr. Sody. And once again asks her not to save him. Dr. Sody and the psychologist persuade her that he must be saved.

The doctor writes on a sheet of paper: schizophrenia. She counts out the tablets. The aunt signs with a fingerprint to confirm her consent to the treatment. Have they convinced her? Her head is drooping, her eyes are fixed on the table—as these people from Phnom Penh are telling her to do something, there's no option, she'll do it. She'll give her nephew the tablets, just as the important doctor lady is asking, dissolved in water.

The American wife? She must have heard about her husband's

madness. Did she love him? She sent her relatives here to see what had become of him. The aunt took the emissaries to the banana grove. They had a look. They went away. The wife has never shown up here. Fake or not, what does it matter now?

Dr. Sody never looks us in the eyes.

"You've got everything about me here in writing," she says, handing me an A4 sheet printed on one side: a color photo of her and an interview. Four questions, four short answers. A few relevant thoughts: we are all equal, just as capable, strong, and hard-working. Both men and women. Women shouldn't be afraid of life. Women change the world by working hard and should be valued just as much as men. The interview was given to mark International Women's Day, 2014.

We have some questions for Dr. Sody, too. About her start in life: she was born in 1955 in Siem Reap, and she had a twin brother. They were the youngest of seven siblings. Their father was a street trader. Their mother stayed at home with the children. The parents realized that education was important. Dr. Sody went to school when she was six years old. So much for her childhood. No details, no fond memories. Two sentences about her older sister: she became a doctor three regimes ago, in King Sihanouk's day. She was a pediatrician, she set an example, pointing the way.

After Sihanouk came General Lon Nol. It was during his regime, in 1974, that, Dr. Sody arrived in Phnom Penh to study medicine. A dreadful time. In the capital, which several years earlier had had a population of one million, there were now two million people. Most of the new million were refugees from the countryside, especially from the east of Cambodia, where

Vietnamese communists were smuggling weapons along the so-called Ho Chi Minh Trail from the north of Vietnam to the south. The Americans dropped 539,000 tons of bombs on eastern and central Cambodia—almost three-and-a-half times as many as on Japan during World War II. They killed thousands of people, though no one knows the precise figures. Anyone who was able to fled into the jungle, which gave no shelter. The safest place was the capital. Or so people thought. Badly bombed, the country was taken over by the black-shirted Khmer Rouge, road after road, town after town, province after province. Those who objected to the collectivization of farmland or who wore glasses were killed—unless they managed to escape to starving Phnom Penh. For months the Khmer Rouge besieged the city, bombarding the suburbs and the center, and laying mines along the Mekong River. The last river convoy carrying food reached the capital on January 26, 1975. Air drops organized by the Americans (providing six hundred tons of ammunition and four hundred tons of rice each day—half of what was actually needed) were suspended in mid-March. People were dying of hunger, or in fires caused by saturation shelling. And from lack of medicine, and from lack of doctors, most of whom had fled to Thailand on the last planes out.

On April 17, 1975, Pol Pot's furious partisans entered Phnom Penh. They drank the water from toilet bowls, thinking they were springs. They ate the toothpaste they found in city bathrooms. They organized the evacuation of the city. Also of the hospitals, including twenty thousand patients. The psychiatric patients were killed on the spot. A large number of books describe how, in just a few days, the city of two million became silent and deserted. There are thousands of detailed accounts of the citizens leaving Phnom Penh. Dr. Sody says nothing about that time. Would she have to search her memory? Spend a few minutes thinking about herself, take up a few minutes of our time? She's clearly uncomfortable. She asks us not to call the four years of genocide (1975-1979) the dictatorship or the regime of the Khmer Rouge. Everyone here is Khmer. It's easy to misunderstand. Let's talk about the time of Pol Pot.

She was living in the countryside, like everyone else, with no guarantee of survival from one day to the next. Fear? Hunger? Exhaustion? Not a word about that. She worked in the rice fields, and cut down bamboo in the jungle for construction work. Her older sister? With her. Dr. Sody hid the fact that she was a doctor because education carried the risk of death. In any case, people knew she could treat their children. They'd come and ask her to save them. But it was impossible, because there was no medicine and no food. What about her other siblings, and their parents? They survived. Apart from her twin. And that's all she says. Not a word more.

Sometimes we go on the road without Dr. Sody. We visit people who live in barracks, in the jungle, in graveyards, by the lake, by the roadside or by the sewer. We're taking a look at how they live. In Battambang, someone has told us to go to Thma Puok. And today we set off at midnight. Along straight, new asphalt through the rice fields, which lie flat to the left and right; the higher up the map we travel, the further they stretch to the horizon. There are fewer and fewer cars, and fewer people. It's a two-hour drive from Battambang to Thma Puok. On the way there everything is green and beautiful. In the town everything is low, gray, and lethargic, entirely transparent somehow, both houses and people, nothing holds our attention for more than a second. Following the directions we've been given, we turn left at the bank, a three-story building—in other words the tallest one here—just as uninteresting as the rest of the place. Then we go right, down a narrow gravel road, where again there's more greenery, nature, countryside. We enter an open yard. The woman who lives here notices us, quickly grabs a colored sarong, runs to the shed and to the woman who's sitting inside it, and tells her to cover herself.

Come here, darling, and I'll rip off your head! It's all right, come to Auntie, I won't do you any harm. Hand your Auntie this, hand her that . . . Apparently the sick woman tries to kill children. Every child she sees. Her parents have brought lots of dry, thorny branches up to her shed. The children throughout the village are reminded on a daily basis: she's like a wild animal, you mustn't go near her. Even the smallest child, who can barely walk, instantly understands the warning, because the sick woman whinnies like a wild horse, howls like a wolf, or roars like a tiger. The voices of illness, which we can hear too. It's impossible to calm her down, nobody even tries. There's no way of communicating with her, but she can see us, she's staring at us, plainly excited to have visitors. She shouts nonstop, the words make no sense, they're vulgar; she may be trying to say we're handsome. That's what our interpreter tells us—he's dismayed. She hasn't moved for three years, her mother tells us. "On that rusty chain. It's ten feet long. She can walk around a bit. But she doesn't want to. She sits naked. At first she still put on a shirt and wrapped a sarong around her hips. Now she spends her life naked. She never sleeps. As if her brain can't understand that her body needs sleep. She sings at night, She never washes. A bucket would be dangerous for her. And for us. She defecates on the spot. I give her water in a plastic bottle. Every morning, before my husband and I go to the fields, I throw some boiled rice onto the floorboards. I scatter it, like for a hen. A plate? A bowl? She might hit me with a bowl. Or injure herself. I don't know if she eats the rice, or if the rats do. She can go for several days on end without eating. She only gets strength from the illness. That's why her ribs are sticking out. That's why she'll die soon."

It looks likely: she can't weigh more than sixty-five pounds, she's a skeleton dressed in skin. A state the doctors would call cachexia. She's thirty-three years old, with long, straight hair on half her head. She has torn out the rest of it, her skull half bare. We call her the Bald Singer. And we learn her name: Chroep.

Seven years ago she finished twelfth grade, went through teacher training, and passed her teacher's exam. Intelligent, quick-witted, and cheerful, she was just about to start work at a school. She loved children. She would have probably been married soon because she was dating a boy—he was educated, well-organized, in love. "One day," says her mother, "we came home from the field, hungry. Our daughter was supposed to be making the dinner. But she wasn't here, and she didn't come back that night. She'd gone missing. We spent a week looking for her, until a monk from the pagoda at Battambang called our local authorities—clearly she was still able to say she'd come from Thma Puok, from the north. What had happened? She couldn't say. So off we went. We put our daughter in a taxi. She hit me in the face. She broke one of the car windows. We tied her hands behind her back. The doctor at the health center, here, in our town, didn't say what was wrong with her. But he clearly knew, and gave her some injections. After them she slept for three days. He promised that in three months things would be better. But it got worse. She was biting people, hitting them. The day she seized a knife—three years ago, the time has flown by—we decided to lock her here in the shed. Lots of people came to help us. Or rather, to watch as my husband and I tied up our own child. She was strong, she struggled and screamed, enough to make the policemen run away. I wouldn't wish this sort of thing on any mother. Such a dreadful worry. Having to sentence your own child to life on a chain. Having to listen to her whimpering day after day. It would be better for the child to die, because then at least there's an end to it. A hard blow, and then you go on living. We've grown accustomed to death here. Malaria, landmines, in mere seconds a person goes up in smoke. One hard blow. And I'd hold a ceremony, I'd pay the monks for the ritual, the child's spirit would be off and away, and might even come back healthy after a time. But no such luck. Daily torment, my daughter's eyes, a curse, a pang of conscience, because when I look at her chain, I feel safe. Am I afraid of my own child? It's agony. As if someone were sticking a knife into me every day of the week. And a burning pain in my chest when the sun's blazing. At night it's like an invisible band around my head, tightening. As if not she, but I were the prisoner. All because of shame, and anxiety. I didn't know how to deal with my daughter's illness. But whenever I hear about a doctor, or a kru, or someone trained abroad, I'd immediately hope he'd be better than our local doctor. I'd take my daughter off the chain, and we'd go for help. I don't believe in evil spirits as strongly as my neighbors do. I've always believed it has to be curable. We've been all over the country. We've been to Siem Reap, Phnom Penh, Ratanakiri, Mondulkiri, and the Cardamom Mountains. Each doctor demanded a lot for his advice. They prescribed herbs, leaves, roots, finely chopped branches. Tablets, various kinds and colors. Or nothing, and just told her to drink more water. A year ago, one of them gave my daughter some white pills that made her entirely lose control. She was foaming at the mouth. So I took her off the pills. For a year she hasn't taken anything. For a year she's been roaring like a tiger, sniggering like a monkey."

"Why is our daughter sick?" her father asks of his own accord. "Just after finishing school she was hit by a motorbike. She fell onto her back. Not her head. The doctors in Battambang X-rayed her spine. They said she'd be fine."

"Maybe the illness was in her from birth?" wonders the mother. "Or did she inherit a dislike of the world from us?"

In Pol Pot's day, the father worked at a quarry. Pol Pot killed ten of his closest relatives. Their spirits don't show up here. It's too far for them. Clearly, they're suffering in the place where they died, unable to rest. Their names, faces, and voices are blurred in oblivion. Later on, he served in Hun Sen's army and fought against Pol Pot. Every step meant the risk of a landmine. Today he tells us about the mines; he remembers his friends being torn apart by them.

What was that about genetic memory? Does the mother wonder about it? Is that what she's telling us? About the biology of fear? About the inheritance of battlefield syndrome?

"When you're ordered to haul earth for four years," she says, "you have to unlearn memory. Unlearn how to think forever.

How to feel? They couldn't teach me not to feel. But not feeling anything would be useful now."

They married after the Pol Pot era. Chroep is their oldest daughter. They have two more daughters, and a son. All three have gone out into the world. Five grandchildren. Their daughter-in-law met someone else in Thailand, so she and their son divorced. Their child, a boy, is now three years old and he lives here, with his grandma and grandpa. Anyway, he lived here before the divorce too. That's common in Cambodia: the parents assign one child, usually the oldest, to care for the grandparents. They hand the child over to them when it's little. They visit once a year. And now the son makes an annual visit from the neighboring province. He went there in search of work; he's a carpenter and earns five dollars a day. He doesn't send any child support.

Dr. Ang Sody? Chroep's parents have never heard of the doctor from Phnom Penh. We're going to do our best to bring her here. Will it be in time?

A million victims of genocide. In January 1979 the Vietnamese army drove the Khmer Rouge into the jungle. The survivors went back to their homes, or occupied those of others. They started searching for their relatives. There was nothing to eat. Over the next few months, another half million people died—of cholera, malaria, and beriberi. And there was no peace for the next twenty years. But a year after the so-called liberation, before the restoration of money, which Pol Pot had abolished, the Medical Academy was opened in Phnom Penh. It was the new country's first college of higher education. The teachers included Vietnamese and Soviet doctors, and a few Cambodian survivors.

Ang Sody was one the first students. There were lectures in the evenings and hospital work in the mornings, because of the lack of doctors. Only seventy in the entire country had survived, so Sody was already treating patients as a student.

Seven years later, when she finished her medical studies, she immediately began to teach others. In the evenings she had students, in the mornings patients. She treated legs, hearts, lungs—the only thing she didn't know how to treat was heads. And those heads were still full of killing, torture, landmines, famine, dying children, back-breaking labor, and panic. With what was left of their reason, the survivors—instinctively perhaps—did their best not to let their hysteria show. In their experience, displaying emotion got you killed. Fear was stifled, sorrow suppressed. Many committed suicide. Dr. Sody had no idea how to help them. Nobody did. Before the genocide there had been two French-educated psychiatrists working in Cambodia. After it, there were none. And among the new doctors, Dr. Sody was probably the only one who understood what mental illness was. She'd read about it in French professional literature. Everyone else thought it was possession—black magic, says her colleague and now boss, Dr. Chhim Sotheara, director of the TPO. "We believed in spirits," he says. "We used to send the patients to folk healers."

One day in 1994, someone at the Khmer-Soviet Friendship Hospital said that some Norwegians had arrived from Oslo University and were looking for doctors interested in studying psychiatry. They needed someone who spoke English.

"Me!" cried Dr. Sody.

Of sixty candidates the ministry selected ten: Sody, and nine men. Doctors with other specializations called them "the crazy doctors." "I still remember their raucous laughter," says Dr. Sody, the country's first female psychiatrist. "But that soon stopped when they had to bring their patients to us. In every family there was someone who'd survived but hadn't returned to life."

Even today, before Dr. Sody finds them in the countryside, the patients are taken to traditional doctors, who, as we know by now, come in various guises. There are herbalists, shamans, folk healers, whisperers, and exorcists. The diagnosis is possessed, enchanted, or cursed. A good traditional doctor can say who cast the spell—which "black magic man" has placed a razor blade or a needle in the sick person's body. To deal with these invisible sharp objects there's an instant need for white magic. Otherwise the victim will die. But a black magic man is best avoided. At one time, some people—as the Khmer country folk still remember— interpreted this warning in a different way: they killed the sorcerer. That used to happen more often, but nowadays they're more aware; in other words they know you can go to prison for that. So how can you help the victim of black magic? The recommendations are: cut off the head of a black or white hen, and leave its body under a tree as a sacrifice to appease the evil spirits. They can eat it up. Other things that can help you deal with insanity-causing black magic—and for any other disorder, too—include a wild pig's teeth, ivory, other animal bones ground or broken into small pieces, the gall bladder of a cobra, holy water, and raw egg—all of which the traditional doctor spreads by hand on the sick person's toes.

"We don't discourage traditional medicine," says psychologist Seang Leap. "If people believe something can help them, why not let them go ahead? As long as it's safe to do so. Sometimes it's not. In one village, a healer made an infusion out of several pounds of chilies and forced the patient to inhale it. He wanted to gas the spirit inside him. Instead he gassed the patient. Another folk healer told a man to drink water from a puddle, to drive out the demon by vomiting. That patient didn't survive either. We explain to people that they shouldn't do that. It's worse if a respected monk recommends a therapy that's dangerous to life or limb. We don't get in the way of the monks. We can't say: 'What he's telling you to do is dangerous.' People will stop listening to us. So we say: 'Pouring boiling water on a sick person's head can weaken the effect of our pills. Don't do the hot water for a month, even better for two.'"

We're in the rainy season, the sky is like steel, it pours for hours at a time; then the sun blazes down, there's sharp light outside the windows, air conditioning inside the car, we're sneezing, and the phone of Leap, the psychologist, rings in his pocket. He looks at the unfamiliar number, answers it, puts a hand over one ear, and with the other listens to someone's voice. "Yes," he says—the conversation is in English. "Sokni is one of our patients. Yes, he's in a cage. What did she say? I didn't hear you. Would you repeat that? That's lucky. We're just on our way to see him. We'll swing by your clinic for a chat. See you soon."

"Listen to this!" says Leap. "Apparently we took money for treating a patient. Sokni's grandmother told the American volunteer about it. The American wants a prompt explanation from us."

"You're joking," says Dr. Sody, clutching her gray head.

The American woman works at the rural health center in

Bavel. She greets us with a wide, bright smile. She looks under thirty. She's wearing a white lab coat, though she's neither a doctor nor a nurse. She's an educator. We want to ask her what she teaches here, and to whom, but she asks the questions.

Dr. Sody explains the first principle of the TPO: *no money.*

Sokni is suffering from schizophrenia. He's been receiving treatment for over two years. In other words, ever since the TPO started breaking chains. They were able to do it because His Royal Highness Norodom Sihamoni, the King of Cambodia, donated five thousand dollars to the organization. The king is deeply concerned about the incarcerated patients; unfortunately he isn't very wealthy, nor is he in charge of the state budget, but he gave as much as he could. Now there's not enough money to liberate them, and the state won't give a single cent to help, so if the American woman knows of an organization that would assume the care of at least a few of the patients, Dr. Sody would be happy to hand them over. Because she's not able to reach all of them as often as she would like. And she has to keep looking for new ones, the ones waiting somewhere behind their houses, tied up in the undergrowth.

"No, no," replies the volunteer. "I don't know of any such organization. I've only been in Cambodia for three weeks. I'm just asking. Sokni's taking some yellow tablets. What are they called?"

The doctor patiently answers each question. The American makes a note of each answer. The orange tablets? And what about the green ones? The people in the village like him, he's a fine boy, but won't he be a danger to his neighbors if he's released? Can his grandma let him go?

The doctor holds her breath, frowns, and then smiles.

"She should. It's not legal to imprison someone with impunity."

"Yes, yes," says the volunteer, also laughing.

The regulations are clear: nobody except a court is authorized to deprive anyone of freedom. Including those who are sick. The reality is different: the authorities tolerate this sort of incarceration, and sometimes encourage it. The TPO tries to persuade the relatives to liberate the patient, but never exerts pressure. The family frees them, not the specialists. "We can only suggest opening the cage or removing the padlock from the chain," says Dr. Sody. "It usually works, and it'll probably work in this case, too."

Leap adds that the grandmother may be keeping her grandson locked up, although he's already on the road to recovery, because she makes a minor profit out of it. Someone will come to see her, reporters from Europe for instance, they'll sit on the kre, have a chat, feel moved by her poverty, and leave a green banknote or two.

"Let's be off now," says Dr. Sody, rising from her chair. "Goodbye."

The wooden hut is hidden in the bushes at the dead-end of the road. This road runs off the highway that people take from the city of Battambang toward the Thai border. Anyone who doesn't know about the cage won't notice it. Sokni won't call out to people. For some time he hasn't been shouting. The brown river babbles nearby, and dense trees rise up behind the bushes, giving plenty of shade, but even so it's as hot as inside a brick oven at his grandma's home today. What about the old lady? She's bowing low.

The psychologist says something to her in Khmer. A few calm sentences. She apologizes to him—she was misunderstood by the American woman. And to Dr. Sody? She doesn't stop for an instant, she doesn't say hello, she just goes directly behind the house, to Sokni. The two women know each other well.

Sokni has been in his cage for fourteen years. Six-and-a-half feet by four, and six-and-a-half feet high, it stands on pillars less than two feet above the ground—or rather, above what he has been excreting.

The grandmother is just over eighty, the grandson just over thirty.

They see each other three times a day: at seven in the morning, when Sokni is given rice or rice soup. At ten, when he's given rice. And in the afternoon, around three—rice. He eats it all with relish, the old lady tells us. "He never complains, he has no favorite dishes. Anyway, I don't know, we don't talk, what would we talk about? That I am old and afraid to open his cage? He was a good child, gentle. The first of the siblings. How many grandchildren do I have? His mother gave me five. The youngest granddaughter is sixteen. She has never come to see her brother. So what if she was born to a different father? She should still visit."

Sokni's father died twenty-five years ago of malaria. And his mother? Yes, Sokni does have a mother. She's sick, too, she was also locked up for several years. Here, in the house. But a year ago the old lady set her free because the medicine brought by the doctor from Phnom Penh helped. Now her daughter doesn't spend her nights in this house, she lives with relatives. She comes by once a week to clean up beneath her son's cage.

The old lady will say a little more about her own husband. Let his life be recorded too. But she tells us about his death: he jumped into the river, because his boat full of rice was sinking. He was drowning. And he almost did. His head was underwater for too long. In vain they dragged him out, in vain. For six months he never woke up. Then he died. Before the war, before Pol Pot. "I only mention it," says the old lady, "so visitors will know. I escaped with the children because there was fierce fighting around here, they ran around firing and shouting, I didn't know who was killing whom, there were bombs exploding everywhere, the river was on fire. When? How should I know the dates? Do you think I can read? I'm grateful to Pol Pot's soldiers because they let us sleep."

At these words the neighbor comes in and sits on the kre. In Cambodia, a neighbor always joins the conversation with visitors without being invited, like a sort of bugging device delegated by the village. And he listens. He corrects the old woman—he knows better where she wandered for the four years of genocide. He gives different details, different names. It's of no significance. What interests us is Sokni.

"Sometimes he dances in his cage," says his grandmother. "He sings, pulls himself up on the bars, tries to pass the time somehow. He caught malaria on a bean plantation just across the Thai border. He had a fever. He didn't know who he was. A spirit took a liking to him. They brought him here. The fever passed, but the spirit remained. Sokni used to go out onto the road, he beat up the neighbors, he stole, he was capable of pinching telephones, the police came and told me to keep an eye on him, they advised me to lock him up. So we put him on a chain. He was a strong boy, he broke free. So with the help of our more distant family we built the cage."

Has she ever taken her grandson to a hospital? "Never"— she's sure of that. "Who'd earn enough for a hospital? We've only a small field, like the plot by the house. We went to a doctor once, I don't know what kind, but he told me to wrap Sokni's head in blankets as a way of boiling the spirit. So we wrapped it again and again, but it did no good at all. Until finally, two years ago, the doctor lady came from the city. Soon after, Sokni stopped shouting."

And today he doesn't say a word.

Dr. Sody has been silent for the past hour too. We're on our way.

Today Dr. Sody wants to show us the main hospital in Siem Reap province. The senior psychiatric registrar here is her former student, who is sure to be willing to tell us what the state-funded psychiatric care is like. The main entrance to the hospital grounds is probably seen by every tourist who comes to visit the nearby Angkor temples, and who stays the night in the city—two-and-a-half million people each year. The hospital gates are at the top of Pub Street, where there's a noisy party every night. Beer, wine, "happy hours": "happy" cocktails, "happy" pizza, and anyone looking for a "happy ending" can find one in the vicinity too. Beyond the bright hospital wall there's a quiet drama going on. Every building is full of patients. Indigent people crowd around the beds and sleep on the floor. They're the patients' relatives. There are no staff to help the patients with their hygiene. There are no hospital meals. The family helps with going to the toilet, and they wash and feed the patients too. And must go outside in the morning when the doctors make their ward rounds. We have arrived at one of these moments. The sun's blazing, the tired crowd is staggering around beneath the trees, lying on the ground, or sleeping. The psychiatric ward? In the building furthest from the gate. Past the TB patients, past HIV. There, on the ground floor, just beyond the entrance, in a bright, square hall there are chairs in rows, like in a theater. All occupied. At the front of the hall are two desks. Behind the desks sit the doctors.

"This is our psychiatric ward," the smiling registrar greets us. "Though there's no ward. Just a corridor. Some of the provincial hospitals don't even have a cardiology ward. This is an outpatients' clinic—you can see what it's like. Fifty patients a day, everyone can hear what the patient says to the doctor, and there's nothing we can do about it. Right now, there's one psychiatrist and one internist working here. I'm the other psychiatrist," says Dr. Sody's former student.

Two psychiatrists for a province of one million people. If someone who's mentally disturbed has to remain in the hospital, they put them in the emergency ward with the victims of car crashes, construction accidents, domestic violence, and feuds between neighbors. Hearing the screams and groans, seeing the blood, the family immediately takes the patient home. Let's not forget: there are fifty psychiatrists working in the whole of Cambodia today, most of them in Phnom Penh. Each day, the doctors see around five hundred patients. They don't have the time for proper diagnoses. They prescribe medicines designed to tranquilize and stupefy. The families often don't have the money to pay for them. Or for further regular treatment, or for other physicians. So they go home, and never return to the hospital.

Untreated schizophrenia, the acute phase of the illness, the psychoses, and other severe mental disorders hidden away in the jungle, in village huts, in the bushes, or somewhere amid the rice fields are Cambodia's national problem. What's the scale, what are the exact numbers? Nobody knows. At the TPO they assume there are at least a thousand patients imprisoned in the villages and small towns, urgently in need of rescue. Possibly two thousand. The majority are suffering from schizophrenia. Over the past two years, Dr. Sody and Leap, the psychologist, have managed to reach seventy patients. They visit each one several times a year.

Or once, and never again.

As today, in the city of Sisophon, on the route from Siem Reap to Battambang. It's the capital of Banteay Meanchey province. Population: two hundred thousand. Wide, dirty, potholed streets, expressionless houses, nowhere with any character, concrete, tin, large billboards everywhere, cadaverous plastic mannequins in the few store windows, and on them some miserable clothes. There are black wires hanging everywhere, trash whirling underfoot, and very few sidewalks, just bare earth corroded by chemicals. There's plastic everywhere, dirt everywhere, a mess everywhere. Outside the pagoda, a man who works for the local Buddhist organization sits down with us. He's a nice, middle-aged man who's concerned about the suffering of others. He can't always help on his own, as in this instance, so he takes Dr. Sody to see those in need.

From the asphalt road we go left, then right, and we're there. A shabby, windowless wooden house stands on posts stuck into a sewer, right beside the red dirt road. When it's dry, the road produces dust that irritates the lungs. When there's a downpour, it changes into a mire.

We're greeted by a sizable crowd. A man in a hat, who looks well over seventy, performs the duties of head of the family. His younger sister acts as mother to the rest. The youngest boy is eight. The oldest daughter is almost thirty. She's the one who's sick. Her name is Kimchi.

Neither the mother nor the father is here with them. "Mom has gone to the hospital in Battambang with a severe pain in her chest," they say. Two days ago she boarded the bus. And she'll come back on the bus. So they all hope. "Was it a heart attack?" the children ask the doctor. Dr. Sody smiles amicably; she's never seen their mother, and has no information about her, so she can't answer. But she finds some words of comfort: if she went on her own, she'll get back on her own.

What about the father? He was old, close to sixty. In Cambodia that's a venerable age. He died a few years ago. Diabetes. So the man in the hat tells us, the mother's brother, uncle of all those assembled. The whole family is sitting on a sloping platform stretched between the red roadway and the entrance to the house. It looks like a gangway leading onto a ship. But this ship is never going to sail anywhere, it'll never sail faraway seas. The passengers won't be moving away from here. Poverty is an anchor that won't let the poor break free. Mom will return here too, alive or dead. There's no way out of poverty. It's a good thing that at least the Buddhist organization operates around here. It gave Mom the money for her ticket and for several days' treatment. It funds one daily meal for the entire family. They go to the pagoda every day at noon for it. They're given takeout for the sick woman; she sits in the dark house, chained to a floorboard. Now she's outside the house with her siblings, on the sloping walkway, because the uncle has allowed them to remove the padlock from his niece's chain for our visit, and bring her into the daylight, into the fresh air, into the stink of burning plastic.

Dr. Sody examines her carefully: a feeble body, trembling, poorly dressed. Her arms and legs are like sticks. Her head is drooping, her hair tangled, long, hiding her face. We can't see her eyes. Can Kimchi see us? There's no contact.

"They sometimes give us good food at the pagoda," says the uncle, "sometimes not so good. We're not complaining. We have no choice. We live off collecting trash. Cans, plastic bottles. Five of us usually work together, from morning to evening, with a break for lunch, by dusk we gather up enough between us for one dollar, sometimes a dollar-and-a-half. My brother-in-law used to bring in the most, but he's no longer here. I am a bachelor, with my sister all my life. It's a good thing my brother-in-law and I managed to put up this house before he died. Look, we've even got a small latrine, four concrete rings, it all soaks into the ground, that's to say into the swamp under the house. We buy drinking water, at a cost of eight dollars a month. A man has to drink, you know. We came here around ten, maybe fifteen years ago, from another place—that one wasn't ours either, and someone drove us out: 'Fuck off everyone, as fast as you can, get the fuck out of here! It's going to be a construction site!' And we ended up here instead. We asked the village chief which spot we could occupy, we'd take any place at all, as long as it didn't belong to anyone. He showed us this stinking gutter. And someone could drive us out of here too at any moment. Before that? We lived in refugee camps, near the border, before the end of Pol Pot. And for fourteen years after him. Because war doesn't end when it ends, you know. First we lived on the Thai side, then on our side. The oldest girl was born in the camp. She was six years old when she fell sick with Dengue fever. Headache, high temperature, then strange behavior. She started shouting, throwing stones at cars, at dogs, and at children. The doctor at the camp said she was different, and she'd never be the same again. Black magic? Possession? My sister and I don't believe in such things. The monks told us there's no black magic. It's an illness. Maybe because my sister felt afraid throughout her own childhood? A refugee camp, too cold, too hot, too damp, poor food, uncertainty, longing. Before that, you know, there was Pol Pot. Of course I remember Pol Pot, I turned fifty a week ago. I was a determined child. The trucks used to take people off somewhere, and we all knew they weren't coming back again. We were all afraid who'd be next. I was too small to work, but I got big enough for school. Except nobody ever saw a school there. Then at the camp I learned to form letters, to this day I can read what's written on the wall over there. But I can't write a single word. Can my sister? She can't read. And the children have never been to school at all. They can't read or write. That's why we're poor. Because of Pol Pot, because of the refugee camp, that's why we're so ignorant. Nobody ever told us we should learn. Nobody sent us to school, nobody gave us a hand."

Who wrote those black letters on the wall of the house? Someone educated helped. What do they mean?

Fucking

drug dealers

no entry!

"That's aimed at my sister's son-in-law. He knows how to read, but what use is it to him, if all he does is steal and cause his family trouble? We have a hard enough time as it is, we can't all work at once, someone always has to stay home with the sick girl."

Why does she spend her life in captivity? Why the chain?

"Because one time she escaped. Sooner or later, a woman who's sick in the head, without protection on the road, will be raped, you know. Plenty are eager to take advantage of an easy opportunity, you know. We can't allow that to happen."

"We know," says Dr. Sody, and poses a few brief questions. The sick woman's uncle provides some brief answers. "She's not sick," says the doctor, concluding the conversation. "She's been retarded from birth. I can't help her."

We're going back to Phnom Penh.

BROKEN COURAGE SYNDROME

The Old Movie House

The capital city stretches across the map, wide and sprawling. Its borders are fluid, which should be taken literally, because it lies below a blue patch named Tonlé Sap. This is a lake that sends water racing from the north toward the metropolis along a river of the same name. And outside the king's palace it crashes into the current of an even wider, even mightier river, the biggest of them all. Into the aorta of Indochina—that's how it's defined in the books. Into the Mother of Waters—that's what they call it here. This is the Mekong, which like every river opens the way for its tributaries without obstruction, but only when its waters are low. Because when the dry season is replaced by downpours greater than anywhere else on earth, when torrid May is replaced by even hotter June, for a moment, for several days, the great river comes to a standstill, falls silent, grows and rises by more than thirty feet, before finally turning around with a roar. Then the Mekong pushes the water back into its tributaries, mostly into the Tonlé Sap river, which spills back into the lake, then the lake's surface rises five times over, reaches the outskirts of the capital, and its three-foot shallows become deeps. Rust-colored, blood-red, fertile gloop floods part of the country. As every year.

Most of the sixteen million Cambodians live on the Mekong and the Tonlé Sap rivers. All but one million are Khmers.

One in three people is under fifteen years old.

The average age is twenty-five.

People over sixty-five account for slightly over four percent of the entire population.

Almost half the pregnant women are anemic because they usually eat less than before they were pregnant: they think that if the baby's too large, they'll have a difficult birth. Many women don't give birth in the hospitals but at rural health centers. Or at home.

Of every one hundred thousand women who give birth, one hundred sixty die.

Among children under five years of age, one in five suffers from malnutrition. One in three is too small.

Over ninety percent of the children receive the necessary inoculations.

Of every thousand children born, thirty die before their fifth birthday.

One in four of the general population is at risk of poverty, but by world standards is not poor.

One in seven is poor; their daily budget is less than two dollars.

Almost half the poor do not register the birth of their children.

The rich are a tiny minority. About 1.5 percent of the population can allow themselves to spend twenty-five dollars a day.

The average monthly wage is one hundred twenty dollars. In Phnom Penh it's twice as much. The women earn less than the men.

Two-thirds of citizens aged over fifteen work.

The majority work without a contract.

One in two is employed in agriculture. One in three in commerce and services. One in five works in industry, most often clothing or shoe-making.

Half the adults have elementary education or none at all.

Four percent have higher education. As a result, the management class are often foreigners.

One Cambodian in five cannot read or write.

One in ten is insured.

One in three has access to tap water.

One in two defecates outside their home.

One in five lives in a city.

There are more than two million people in the capital, possibly as many as three million.

Everyone produces trash. The piles of it in Phnom Penh keep growing from sweltering morning to sweltering evening. Vegetables, fruit, rice, noodles, spoiled meat—all rotting away. Here's the first pile, the fifth, the tenth. Three feet high or more. Each one stewing slowly, like goulash. Seasoned in the course of the day by tuk-tuk drivers' urine; after dusk it starts to seethe. Now it's pulsing like a large anthill. But there's no wind. Or streetlamp nearby. Food wrappers, bottles, paper, polystyrene, all of it alive, all stirring in the silence, shimmering in the dark. Hungry dogs? Rats? Cockroaches? You bet! Nowhere here is free of them.

In the daylight, the royal palace looks over the outlet of the Tonlé Sap as it flows into the Mekong. Between the palace and the river is a large empty square, as hot as a frying pan. The locals buy seeds in small plastic cups from peddlers and help their children feed the pigeons. Apart from the river, this is the only wide open space here. It's a pleasant sight, because the entire district is cramped and constricted, at most four or five stories tall. House stands beside house, constructed in the days of the French, once fine-looking, most of them now neglected, like nothing on earth. Cheap and expensive hotels, restaurants, pubs, cafés, wine bars, clubs, a daytime bazaar and a nighttime market. Brothels. Other districts don't usually interest the tourists. Apart from Riverside, there's not much else for them in the city. The Genocide Museum? Otherwise known as Prison S-21 in former Tuol Sleng school, a Phnom Penh tourist attraction a short way from the Riverside district. It's a fifteen-minute tuk-tuk ride to get there, for three dollars, three hours staring into hundreds of pairs of eyes photographed shortly before the end, and three dollars for the ride back. Farther out are the killing fields. The trip there costs more because Pol Pot did his wholesale killing in the suburbs. Anyone who sets off from Riverside to have a look at the skulls returns in the afternoon. The tourists go there and back, take photographs of the monks (which goes against good manners), the sunset over the river; they eat and drink, some stay sober, some get drunk, there's grass to smoke or drugs, whatever you want, whatever you like, there are girls, there are boys, there are children. *Mister, mister, do you want a kiss?*

In Phnom Penh you can buy anything: any life, any death.

The creeping of the warm garbage heaps. Children scavenging in the refuse. Gray and brown, invisible in the darkness. Focused on the job, on sorting the trash. What can they still gain from the pile before the garbage truck comes in the morning? What can they sell, what can they eat? Where do they all live? *All* of them? We don't know. Some are sure to live at the movie house. Like the ones who sell seeds for the pigeons outside the palace. And those who sweep the streets, the architects of the vibrating trash heaps.

The movie house is on Street 130, climbs to a height of five stories, and hasn't been a movie house for years. It's a ticking bomb, the experts will tell you, and those affected pretend they're not bothered. They're not aware of any threat, they've haven't heard a thing, they can't see anything wrong. Like the mother of the guy who drowned in the river close by, at the spot where 130 runs at a right angle into Street 01.

Her son was eighteen, and he worked for the firm that cleans the city, in a team with his mother and some other women. They swept the streets, and collected the trash in a cart that he pushed and emptied at a spot where the garbage trucks drive past. Every day, from four to nine in the morning, and from midday until three in the afternoon. Every day the same five crossroads, the same junctions, the same children. "That day, after work, my son went to the river to bathe," the mother tells us. "People were watching and laughing, they thought he was fooling around, but he was shouting because he was drowning."

The water seized her son. It never gave him back. The mother employed the best people to search for him—meaning the Vietnamese. They live by the river, they know its eddies better than anyone. They took five hundred dollars each for a day's search. Once she had spent the three-and-a-half thousand she'd borrowed, she said: "Stop! I can't go on looking for my son."

Although she hadn't found the body, she had to hold a funeral: one thousand dollars for the pagoda for all the funeral requisites, smoke, aromatics, and holy monastic rituals. And almost as much again for a reception for the neighbors. She can't have left enough money at the pagoda, because her son comes back to her at night, Momma, he cries, Momma, plainly he hasn't gone far away, he's still wandering the streets he used to sweep, in the daytime too, wet and frozen because the sun freezes him, he also shows up at the movie house, he still has some business here, he climbs all the way to the roof to his mother, but he never stops, he never rests. On the anniversary of his death she'll have to ask the monks again—maybe this time they'll facilitate her son's onward journey.

Like every mother in the world who has lost a son, the woman who lives on the roof now says he was a good boy, hard-working, as everyone knows, didn't drink or smoke, even knew how to write because he finished elementary school. It's been almost seven years since he sank into the deep. Hopeless. The mother doesn't sweep the streets anymore. She sells eggs on the nearest corner. Her husband, the boy's father, pays a dollar to rent a rickshaw for seven hours. He carries tourists, who always haggle. Everything the drowned boy's parents earn goes toward repaying their debts. Their tin shack on the roof of the movie house is the most luxurious place in the building. Sometimes there's a draft of air from the river. There's even a toilet. The sewage runs down to who knows where, but where else is it to go?

What sort of luxury is this? The rain drips on their heads, and they have nothing to patch the ceiling of the tin shack. Because they still have to pay for their younger daughter's treatment. For what? Who here would question the doctors? Who would dare? The doctors haven't explained anything, they've just told them she needs a transfusion every few days. Two hundred dollars a time. Here at the movie house everyone's sick. Nobody has the money for doctors. Here at the movie house, everyone's in need of everything. From the street, where we can only see its facade, the movie house looks like a movie house. But in fact it's a slum.

The building, in Khmer brutalist style, dates back to the

1950s. The name of the movie house is Hemakcheat. The auditorium on the second floor was vast—apparently it held a thousand seats. In the 1960s, often referred to as the golden years of Khmer culture, the citizens of Phnom Penh used to flock to the movies. They watched American and French productions, but also Cambodian ones. Hundreds of movies were made here in those days. Several directed by King Sihanouk himself. Until April 1975, when the movie house on Street 130 closed down, when the whole city closed down.

Four years later, the Khmer Rouge left and people returned to the city. Country folk arrived too because their land had been ripped up by bombs. They came to the city in search of a better life, and they found the movie house. They removed the seats from the auditorium, and moved in. The smarter ones settled higher up, in the office rooms. Each room had an entrance from an outer gallery.

That's still the case today. On the first floor, beyond the former main entrance on Street 130, there was once the main lobby, including the ticket desks. Now there are no ticket desks. And those people are gone. There's nobody hurrying to see a screening. Inside the lobby, motorbikes wait for their owners, in neat rows, packed in tightly, five hundred riels goes to the parking attendant for each one. We too leave our scooter here when we go inside the movie house that isn't a movie house. We go out into the street again, and along the left side of the building. We tread cautiously on the narrow, wet concrete that leads down an ever-gloomier passage the entire length of the side wall, which is on our right. On our left there's another building; typical for Riverside, it's close, at most ten feet from the movie house. In the wall of the movie house—we're still at street level—there are several open doors into tailor's workshops. Here, in these dark lairs, seamstresses are working by feeble lamplight. We keep walking until we reach the back wall. There the passage ends in a stairwell, which has a window, so it's a bit brighter. Everything's dirty, greasy, every step sticky. We're going inside.

On the landing level: the first door, the first apartment, five feet high. A young woman lives here with her child. Higher up there's a communal toilet and the end of the stairwell. Now we must go out onto the narrow outer gallery, a balcony stretched the entire length of the side wall of the building. On the gallery there's a tangle of blue plastic pipes and some blue plastic hoses; people do their bathing here, so it's always noisy, wet, and slippery. The water drips on the heads of those who enter from the street. To the left of the hoses there's a narrow door into the auditorium, dark as a bottomless cave. In the daytime, separate rays of light fall in here through small holes in the outer wall. This also provides ventilation. But not enough. The movie house stinks like a fresh mass grave. This is where the poorest people live. No living conditions could be worse. Little huts, shacks. One family in each. Two generations, or three. Though three is rare, because life in the movie house isn't long. People are cooking something, eating something, pretending they can't see the mound.

But the black mound is right there.

Every day for the past forty years it has been growing, it's alive, pulsating. The tenants have been building it ever since they moved in here: garbage, bones, and if you were to rummage well, you'd find human fetuses, the remains of children, the remains of adults. The mound keeps gaining strength, accumulating life, imposing rules, and inducing evil. Inside lurks every despair; no criminal, no outsider will enter this cave. No prosecutor, no policeman. Everywhere is slippery, the whole floor is throbbing, cockroaches, rats run around your feet, or they swim between your legs in the rainy season. Here, too, water drips onto people's heads. And above their heads are bats, they're always flying around in here, whatever the time of year. At any moment the floor that carries the living mound could crash down on the woman who lives with her child half a story below. And onto the motorbike parking lot.

Outside the door into the auditorium there's a little air again, and we go back to the gallery. Near the blue plastic hoses there's an external metal staircase, the steps are one person wide, rusted through, full of holes—some we have to jump across. We're going higher, to the third floor. There's a balcony the length of the building here, too, but instead of one entrance into the auditorium there's a row of doors, room after room. And then more of the same fire stairs, the fourth floor's the same. So is the fifth. Each room is a gloomy cavity, where the only light enters through the door and a window just next to it. But only if there's glass in the window, because usually there are boards. It's easier to live here than in the auditorium. Outside the doors the sun is shining, and here you can lie on a kre, breathe in the shade, your neighbors pass by, they give you something to smoke, and bring in gossip from the street. And you don't even have to run down the stairs to the bathroom. The residents in almost every room have built a toilet. They've stuck pipes into the floor. The sewage? It runs into the auditorium, onto the garbage mound, onto their neighbors' heads.

Recently the city authorities asked a Czech NGO to test whether the mound—made out of every kind of human waste material—was safe for people to be around.

Like every village, or every human settlement in Cambodia, the movie house has its head man. The movie-house head is a man named Srey Chhan, age seventy, who has lived half his life here. He was thirty-five when Pol Pot fled Phnom Penh and escaped into the jungle. It was at that time that Srey Chhan took over part of the auditorium by the outer wall; he made a large hole in it, and built a plywood partition around it—now entirely covered in mold—to separate himself from his neighbors. He likes the fresh air. He has four adult children, his daughters have been married off, his sons sleep here, all four work on construction sites. His wife? She died two years ago, her blood pressure was too high. At first she was in the hospital for a while, but she had to come back here because the doctors were too expensive. "And she died here," her widower tells us, "we all die here, old and young, and very tiny. Sometimes you can hear mothers wailing in this building, because their child has gone stiff and cold at the breast. And the others? Most often the people here suffer from diarrhea, or a cough, they choke on blood, they swell up like fresh corpses. Some faster, others slower, of course it's because of the mound, what else?" The community chief has no doubt about it. "The mound deals us death, it emanates it, we're all slowly dying because of it."

What about the NGO experts? Some time ago they came to the movie house wearing masks, talked to people, took pictures, then went away, and that was the last anyone saw of them. Everyone knows the mound has to be removed, but how is it to be done? Almost a hundred families live in here, more than three hundred people. The movie house belongs to them. There are documents, it's officially their property.

Why are the city authorities interested in the movie house?

Do they want to warn people about the danger? In Cambodia, no one believes the authorities have good intentions. Every form of authority is against the people. The authorities squeeze every last cent out of them. The people have to sit quietly. Because if they stand up for themselves, the authorities will soon put them in order. The authorities are concerned about land, and this site is the most valuable one in the entire city. Possibly in the entire country. Someone important already has his eye on this site, already wants to make a profit at the expense of the poor residents. He'll probably give them a few thousand dollars each—a semblance of concern for people is important in Cambodia, sign these papers and move on, the sooner the better. In short: fuck off and get lost. The people here have never in their lives seen a few thousand dollars all at once, so they'll take it willingly, they'll sign whatever's necessary, and only then will they wonder where in this city, with that money, will they find a patch of floor, a wall, or at least a pillar under a roof to hang up a hammock.

The Czech NGO asked three construction firms to provide expert opinions. The experts wrote that the mound in the movie-house auditorium is oppressive, toxic, constantly emitting methane. An impending disaster. Some advised removing the mound, others said not to move it, but to demolish the building, mound and all. Either way, the people should be moved out of there as soon as possible.

For now, the people are unaware of this. Or else that's just what they say. Like the childless old couple from the fifth floor. They ended up here when Pol Pot lost power. They took over a room with a door onto the gallery. He managed to get himself a bicycle, and gave people rides. She had a stall selling limes for someone else. That's how they earned the money for their rice.

And now? They collect plastic bottles. They walk around the entire district together, and in a single evening they pick up over thirty pounds of empty bottles. They tie the sack, now taller than a man, to a rope and hoist it up to the fifth floor. In the morning they lower it to ground level, take it to the collection point, and get almost two dollars for it. That's enough to buy food.

The state of their health varies. Two years ago, he slept and slept, he was at death's door, so she asked the neighbors for help. They took him to a traditional healer. "Why are you bringing me a dead body?" snapped the healer; he didn't know how to help. What could they do? They went to the Vietnamese hospital. The doctors took the sick man into the *emergency room* (in Cambodia, English terminology is often used as well), did a lumbar puncture, and confirmed meningitis. For the first day they charged 500 dollars, 400 for the second, and 360 for the third. The patient woke up, so it was worth staying for a fourth day too—220 dollars. Then for the fifth and each subsequent day the cost was 190. He lay there for two whole weeks, then finally got up. The doctor warned his wife that strange things might happen to him, and she must get used to the idea that he might do or say something that wasn't normal. And he does: sometimes he babbles nonsense, and loudly, because he's deaf. But he still has the strength to pick up bottles every evening. How long will he go on like that? Until he doesn't have enough breath to climb to the fifth floor. Then they'll go to the pagoda, like all the old people with no children, or whose children have abandoned them. At the temple the monks will help them, and they'll get a bowl of rice each for washing the floor—maybe there, at least for a short while before death, their fear will leave them.

The fear that never goes away: tomorrow someone will

forbid them to collect bottles, some authority will come along and say it's not allowed. It's a fear of other people. They'll come and shout: "Shut your mouth! Don't speak unless you're asked! And get out of here, scram!"

Are they afraid of the mound that's growing three floors below? "No," say the old couple, "the mound isn't a person. What we're afraid of is the past repeating."

The wife lists their loved ones who were killed by the Americans, or by Pol Pot; it takes a few minutes for her to reel off name after name. It's a fear of having your hands tied behind your back, of being blindfolded, of a sudden explosion. It intensifies whenever a helicopter flies over the city. Or when they show bombing raids on television. A few of the people in the movie house have television sets. At those moments these old folks avert their gaze from the screen, get up, go out into the fresh air, and look at the sky to make sure there are no planes overhead. Because they remember that bombs fall quietly. As quietly as the black mound in the old movie house is growing.

A Metaphor

On the boulevard near the royal palace (on Street 01) we sometimes observe the families who, after a hot and arduous day at work, come to sit on the grass: parents, children, less often grandmothers, even more rarely grandfathers; they have something to eat, and to drink, and they laugh. And we always watch out for that boy, though we've never actually seen him before. That's to say we've only seen him on YouTube—while searching online for one of the NGOs that operate in Phnom Penh we chanced upon a short video that tells the story of a poor teenager with no relatives. In it, the boy wandered among the people relaxing here, asking if anyone wanted to be weighed. A small bathroom scale—that was his only possession, with which he was trying to make a living. He needed the money to buy food and to study. The camera followed him—it must have been somewhere here, on the river—and it showed how nobody reacted to his requests. Nobody wanted to be weighed, nobody gave him a single riel. The story was moving and sad, so now, whenever we spend time by the river, we look out for him and the weighing scale under his arm.

But in months and months we haven't come across him. The Riverside district is large, and the boulevard is long. Finally, we go online to look for that video again. Perhaps a detail will tell us exactly where on the riverbank we should look for the boy with the scale, and at what time of day he usually works. We have no trouble finding the video on Google. It's less than five minutes long. It was made in 2010. There aren't many online views.

"In the morning, I get up, and fold my mat," says the boy in Khmer, and on the bottom of the screen we read the English translation. "I wash my face, then I go downstairs. I pick up some rice and run to school. I study until 10 A.M., and then go back home to clean the house. Then I wait for the others to come and we play music." Then a title appears in the middle of the screen that reads: "Chan Sori, 14 years old, abandoned by his parents."

"These days Cambodian people don't want to learn traditional music," says Sori to the camera, as the screen shows him playing the gong chime. "That's why I'm learning—I don't want to see it disappear. I want to be a musician because my situation is quite tenuous. I cannot further my education, so my only hope is music. I don't ask to be rich. Just to have enough for me and for the family I'll start one day. For us to be happy. After music practice, I change my clothes, pick up my lunch, and go back to school. All my money goes toward food and school. But it's never enough, because I have lots of extra classes and I have to pay for them. So I need a lot of money, but I never have enough. The others at school say I am a fatherless child, and that I'm just a boy who weighs people, so they don't want to play with me. They say I should just go and play with other poor kids like me. They're jealous of me for being a model student. They say, 'How can a boy who weighs people do so well at school?' I hate them!"

"Anyone want to be weighed?" Sori, small, polite, and unassuming, walks along the boulevard, with the camera following him. "Anyone want to be weighed?" Then, to the camera, "A few of my classmates work here too, selling cold drinks, but at least they have their parents—their lives are okay. They don't have it hard like me."

The boy on the screen wipes away his tears and sets off into the city as dusk falls, the scale under his arm. Now we're certain: the building he leaves to go to work is the White Building.

We know this place well, very close to the Mekong, in between the points where two rivers flow into it, the Tonlé Sap and the Tonlé Bassac. In keeping with King Sihanouk's vision, in the late 1950s and throughout the 1960s Phnom Penh underwent great change. A large number of modern public-utility buildings and communal multi-family housing blocks were constructed in this period. There was no alternative, because the capital's population was growing at lightning speed: in 1953 it was 370,000, but by 1970 it was one million. One of the king's ideas at the time was this one, known in English as "Bassac River Front."

It was going to be a riverside cultural district, with schools for the arts, theaters, concert halls, exhibition spaces, museums, and apartments for creative artists and for the middle class. The project was only partly realized. In charge of the work was an urban planner named Vann Molyvann (who died in 2017), the first Cambodian architect to obtain a thorough modern education in France. He was a student of Le Corbusier himself. The influence of the great architectural artist and father of brutalism is easy to perceive in the modernist facade of the White Building, although the French master's Khmer student did not design this particular building himself, but merely oversaw the work. The architects who designed it were the Cambodian Lu Ban Hap and the Russian Vladimir Bodiansky. From the old photographs, it looks as if the building was erected in a wide empty space. It was 984 feet long and contained 468 apartments, into which the tenants moved in 1963. Many of them were professional painters or sculptors, actors, musicians, or dancers.

Many of them never came back from compulsory resettlement.

A small number succeeded. Or their children did. After four years of deafening emptiness and inhuman silence the long block came back to life with the rest of the city. Although various alternative creative types moved in, the place now gained a different reputation: for poverty, violence, theft, prostitution, diseases, booze, drugs, knives, and as a slum. But in time it was known for lots of good things too: education for the children, a library, social and creative projects, the movies, music and dance.

The story of the White Building was presented by the world's leading newspapers and TV channels as a metaphor for tired and battered Cambodia. The White Building hasn't been white for the longest time—its walls are being eaten away by black mold. There are open stairwells linking six modules. The first and last modules have five stories each, and the middle ones have four. The roofs are flat—these large, empty terraces were once probably meant to be gardens. On the floors below there are long, dark passages, with scratched or scorched walls; a row of doors on the left, and a row on the right, heavy security bars on each door with several locks and padlocks, one or two rooms in each apartment, plus an open "room" that has no front wall. Meaning everyone here lives outside, to some extent. The dark passages stink of urine. There are children running around, shouting, playing games, and pomaded teenage girls on the stairs, solemn and proud, hanging over the railings from early morning. Their dolled-up male peers are sprucing their hair. Somewhere nearby some old people are lying down to rest; they have some dreadful memories, and probably aren't interested in life anymore. Adults in ragged, threadbare clothes sit sweating on the grease-coated steps, or lie in hammocks tied to the barriers. Someone's sweeping, someone's cooking, combing their hair, or commenting on our visit. We often stop in here. There are lots of furtive glances, but also welcoming smiles. A mix of idleness and daily anguish.

In the YouTube video, Sori doesn't reveal why he's on his own. He doesn't say a word about it. The title says his parents abandoned him, but this short account doesn't explain the matter. Fountains that change color, bright lights, sad music, the picture fades out, and that's the end. It was produced by a foreign NGO as part of a series called "Kids in the City." Did the video change Sori's life?

We download a few frames showing his face onto a phone. We call one of our interpreters, who works on a daily basis as a motorbike taxi driver—and a few minutes later we arrive at the White Building. We take out the phone.

It doesn't take us long to find Sori. The interpreter proves unnecessary. "The video changed nothing for me," says the boy in fluent English. "They made it when I was a child, and I've just turned eighteen. I'm still living here. And I get up at six, just as I did then. I wash, run down to the street, buy some warm rice, and race off to take these rich people's black dachshund for a walk. At seven I start school—I'm still studying classical Khmer music. Classes go on until eleven. There's a foundation that supports my education, they give me fifty dollars a month, but it's going to end soon because I'm about to finish high school. I take the dachshund out again at four. Then what? I run to the National Museum. I'm there from five to eight, working as an usher. That gets me another fifty dollars, so altogether I earn one hundred a month. Plus twenty for the dachshund. Four dollars a day, it's hard to survive on that in the capital. But I don't weigh people anymore. I spend my spare time playing and dancing in a group. I love art," Chan Sori tells us. "When I'm playing the xylophone or when I'm dancing, my mind is empty. I forget about my life."

When he's not playing, it all comes back: he came to the White Building with his mom when he was five years old. At the time, his father had abandoned them. He can hardly remember his father. He and his mother moved into a room, one floor down, he thinks. They got by. Until one day, when he was thirteen, he came home from school and his mom was gone. She'd run up debts and taken off, vanished. A week later she came back, briefly. She said he should get a weighing scale and find a way to manage. He moved in with the neighbors, but after a few weeks they started quarrelling: they said he was getting in the way, he had to leave. "I was no one's," he tells us, wiping away his tears and apologizing for them. "There's no justification for what my mom did to me."

He's sporadically in touch with her. He visits her now and then, far away in the countryside. He brings her money.

When he left the unpleasant neighbors' apartment, his music teacher came to the rescue, and said he could sleep in a classroom on the building's fourth floor, which until recently had been his own living space, as he and his family had moved out to a better place. Now it's Sori's home: back when the video was taken, and now, as we meet him several years later. Instead of paying rent he has to do the cleaning.

He gets home from the National Museum each evening before nine. There's no kitchen here, and no cooking equipment, so he buys rice from a street vendor, as well as drinking water— the tap water in Phnom Penh isn't fit to drink—goes up to the fourth floor, locks the security bars from the inside, removes the keys from the padlock, switches on a fan, and sleeps. But what's in his dreams isn't a dance, or music. It's the turbulent Mekong.

How's Sori doing now?

We haven't seen him for some time.

And there's bad news from the White Building.

Today, all the residents are frantically running up and down the stairs, shouting, and carrying rags, pots, and stools. Or they're sitting quietly outside their front doors, sad, resigned, inactive. Singly and in whole families. And Sori? We can see his apartment through the security bars. Inside there's not a single piece of equipment, no furniture, none of the posters that used to hang on the walls. *I LOVE ART, Sori,* reads a message in marker on the dado, in his handwriting, so this is undoubtedly his room. Already vacated. The apartment opposite is empty too. Some trash on the floor, some mildewed bits of paper, some rusted cans, a portrait of King Sihanouk that's been gnawed by rats, some faded photos, a broken mirror, a gap-toothed comb, a splayed toothbrush, a broken fork, a cracked glass, a leaking plastic bowl, and an old flip-flop. There's no one we can ask about Sori.

A Japanese firm is going to put up a commercial and office block on the site of the White Building. It'll be tall, twenty-one stories. Each family has been given fourteen hundred dollars for each square yard of vacated property. Anyone who had around 650 square feet, because in the past they'd cleverly joined up two apartments for free, can now buy a house in the suburbs. Anyone who had half that can't buy anything, not even a long way from the city center.

We watch as the White Building community ceases to exist. Truck after truck drives up to the entrance. The residents load all their possessions onto them. Without shedding a single tear, they drive away to who knows where, not knowing if they'll ever see their neighbors again. But they shouldn't complain. There are plenty of buildings in Phnom Penh, including in this neighborhood, whose occupants have been evicted without any compensation at all—because they had no title deeds, but the people who are being moved out today do have them.

Chan Sori didn't have any. We walk about the building, showing his picture. Sori? Which Sori's that? The last few residents are carrying down the remains of their belongings, of their indigent existence. Some men in green overalls are on their way to the upper floors, with hammers and nails. They're nailing each apartment shut, one after another, with rough wooden boards. Corridor after corridor. Finally, the entire building is empty. Five hundred families have gone in five hundred directions. No re-entry from now on. Heavy machinery drives in to demolish wall after wall, floor after floor. Sori? Which Sori? There were lots of Soris here.

Three Outcast Mothers

Number one. In the city she was a garbage collector, here she's nobody, even in her own eyes. She often forgets who she is, she loses consciousness, closes her eyes and opens them; she'll be giving up the ghost soon. We're not to be shocked if she falls on her face. Today she might not. Today her head's better. She knows they call her Kol. She's not sure if it's her first or family name. She's never spent a single hour at school. She gave birth to three sons, and is over forty.

We're sitting outside a gray house made of bricks. It's very hot, and flies are getting into our mouths. Right beside us there's a concrete platform covering some water, or rather what was once a pond, or a very small lake. In Cambodia there's always water flowing somewhere nearby. Or standing. It's wet and boggy everywhere in the rainy season. Because when the sun beats down for months on end, the earth is soon as dry as a bone. The red-hot concrete supports almost the entire settlement. Half the residents are suffering from diarrhea. As one of them starts to recover, another falls ill. Six thousand people with no sewage system.

When they were thrown out of the city, they came here. To

tents that they had to construct for themselves out of plastic sheets, rags, and sticks. A few years later the pond was covered with concrete, and some brick barracks were put up on top of it, all coated in white plaster. There's a row of rooms in each one, each door represents one family. Inside it's cramped and stuffy, so in the daytime life goes on outside instead. Lots of narrow alleyways have appeared on the concrete platform; in front of the barracks are some small stores and stalls selling dried fish. No one removes the garbage from here. People burn plastic. In the evening, lightbulbs shine here and there at the center of this outcasts' settlement. The edges of the settlement are dark—that's where those who couldn't afford a brick room sleep, in shacks knocked together from bamboo poles and tin, on low pillars or in the mud, in the piss. There are too many people displaced from the city. A little further on, a second settlement has been established. And a third, a fifth, a seventh. Brick barracks. Too few barracks. Houses made of sticks.

"Today I can't breathe," says Kol. A devil has taken up residence in her. Because of that new slut of her husband's. She casts spells, performs rituals, and wishes Kol a speedy death. Doctors? What about them? What do they know? They say there's nothing wrong with her, she just doesn't want to be alive. But where's she to get the will to live from? The sun is turning her blind, she doesn't eat much, she hasn't any strength, and she sleeps on concrete in someone else's drab home. With strangers next door. And with her son, who's listening now, as his mom surrenders to death. He's six years old, with an empty stomach. His older brother, aged ten, is not here. The brother lives far away, with Kol's mother. The grandmother needs care, she's almost eighty, she has trouble walking, they haven't seen each other for eighteen months. What do they eat there? Kol has no idea. There's an oldest son too, the third one, he's twenty. He collects trash in Phnom Penh. He comes to see his mother every three months. When was the last time? He hasn't been here for half a year, he doesn't answer her calls, his cellphone must have been stolen. Or someone's done him harm.

"He's free. Be happy," Gap-toothed Grandma tells Kol.

Number two. She's over fifty. With thick, black hair. But she hasn't many teeth left. Gap-toothed Grandma is always laughing. She's as skinny as the local dogs, her arms and legs like sticks. Her children are in jail. The older son got ten years for rape. His younger sister got a lesser sentence because it was for theft. There are two more, the youngest. They go to school, so they aren't here now. Gap-toothed Grandma works in someone else's rice field from dawn to the time when the sun is at its hottest. She earns five dollars a day, enough for two portions of rice for the children and three glasses of rice wine for herself. She likes rice in that form. She has trouble with her memory. But she'll never forget that day in June. The police came at 6 A.M. Clear the houses! They're going to build tower blocks for rich people. Anyone who resisted was clubbed on the back. Everyone resisted. They fired tear gas at the poor.

Gap-toothed Grandma was happy living in the city. In the mornings she worked at the Boeung Keng Kang bazaar on Street 380, near the junction with Street 63. Under a large tin roof—we know the place well—on a stone floor awash with fish or meat slime, the women (less often men) sell rice, vegetables, fruit, seafood, fish, poultry (they kill the fish and chickens in front of the customers), meat, noodles, beer, soap, plastic pails, bowls, and clothing. Alongside there are hairdressers, manicurists, masseuses, beauticians, dressmakers, and fortune tellers at work. And cooks. There's always something to eat at the bazaar. And Gap-toothed Grandma? She was a helper there, fetch, carry, don't expect too much. In the morning, as the bazaar was just opening, and in the afternoon when they were closing up. In between, when the sun was at its hottest, she worked outside. After the stuffiness of the bazaar she liked to breathe the city air. That's to say, exhaust fumes—downtown Phnom Penh is all traffic jams and acrid smoke, from dawn to dusk. She would shield her face and push along someone else's two-wheeled cart, selling snails from the Mekong, and then sharing the earnings with the cart's owner. She liked the traffic, the car horns, she liked watching the well-off people sitting in the cafes. And her husband? He worked on the tall construction sites she passed every day, five dollars for twelve hours, there's construction underway all over the capital now, the city's growing, the rich need penthouses, cubicles for their corporate minions, offices, shopping malls, banks, restaurants, hair salons, car showrooms, and every kind of massage parlor. Except that from here, the settlement for outcasts, it was too far and too costly for her husband to travel to those construction sites. He gave up his job. He developed chronic diarrhea. It'll soon be one year since he died of the shits. Fifty-four years old.

During the past quarter century, one in ten of Phnom Penh's residents has been evicted from their home—so estimate the NGOs—or even one in eight. Usually, this involves a violation of their rights. In other cities it's the same. And in the countryside. Almost a million people have been driven out of their fields and farms. They were forced to make way for large palm sugar and rubber plantations. This was decreed by the authorities, who go hand-in-glove with big business. Cambodia is possibly the most corrupt state in this part of the world. The poorest people are the ones who pay for the authorities' corruption. They're the ones who have to give bribes just about every time they deal with state officials: clerks, doctors, teachers, policemen, customs officers, border guards at the airport, firefighters. Your house is on fire? We'll put it out. But first pay up.

There were also some who had to make way for water because the Chinese are building gigantic dams on the local rivers, and they're flooding villages. The outcasts can't afford much—most of them can't afford anything. They move out further away, often to somewhere by a sewer where nobody and nothing else wants to live.

Number three. Pa moved out to the suburbs of Phnom Penh too. Beautiful, proud, with a powerful, intelligent look in her eyes. She's been sitting with us from the start, listening to her neighbors' complaining. She's the thinnest of them all. She hasn't said a word yet. The photographer asks if he may take her picture. Go ahead, she says, smiling for a second, or maybe three. Someone's noticed her, asked her for something, for a moment something depends on her. Beautiful Pa, aged thirty, lots of illness, no close relatives. She does in fact have an older brother, but he works on a construction site somewhere in Phnom Penh. They haven't met up for years. Her father died when her mother was carrying her in the womb. She has never seen her father's face—he never had his picture taken. She has never dreamed about him. When she reached the age of ten, her mom fell pregnant again, but didn't survive it. Impoverished pregnant women often get infections, they don't have the money for doctors, so it ends badly. As a teenager in Phnom Penh, Pa used to pick up plastic trash and take it to the collection point. Sometimes in a single day she got two-and-a-half dollars for it. Enough to survive. Because at one time plastic was worth something, not like now, just a few cents. When she has less strength, she can barely make two bucks a week. She eats when she finds leftovers on someone's plate, at a café at the bazaar. Life used to be different—she lived on Diamond Island, a short walk from the royal palace. In those days there were some bushes on that site, with paupers' shacks standing among them. One day the people were thrown out, and a new city was constructed on the island, with a triumphal arch like the one in Paris, and a town hall. She came to the settlement with her uncle, her mom's brother. In time he made some money, and built a house nearby. Now he won't even let his niece take a rest outside his garden gate. The uncle is afraid of the diseases Pa's carrying. He tosses half a dollar onto the concrete just to avoid touching her, or letting her breathe on him. He shouts: Get the fuck out of here! What's wrong with her? Pa doesn't know. She has a swollen stomach, heart palpitations, her head's bursting. She's never been to a doctor.

Pa's husband is afraid of her, too. She had a husband and three children. The husband took them all away. He stole them and ran off. At the time, the youngest son had only just started to walk. It's been four years since she last saw all three of them. She doesn't cry, at least not when people are watching. She can't count, read or write, she's never had a calendar or a telephone. She sleeps alone in a leaky shack made of sticks, six feet by six feet, in a puddle, in fear, because it's not her puddle.

Someone's going to chase her out at any moment, someone's going to destroy that shack of hers. "It makes my head spin," says Pa anxiously. The girl in our photograph.

The Mother of Slaves

There's a construction site on almost every street in the capital. In front of each one is a neatly-stacked pile of bricks. They're brought in from the suburbs, where Eth lives.

Eth invites us up to her home. Sometimes a minor landslide occurs here. Her youngest son is two. The clay could bury him. He could be run over by a tipper truck; the drivers sit high up, and won't see a naked brown child against the clay. Sometimes around fifty trucks roll by in the course of a single day, right in front of the house. The earth shakes, the slag heap grows, and you can't see the sky. No grass, no flowers, no greenery. No respite for the eyes. Just clay and more clay. The miserable tin shack of a home stands by the entrance to the brick factory: a wooden floor, four paces square, resting on eight little pillars. Life goes on inside the house and underneath it. You have to bow your head? Lower than that? Because everyone, everywhere here, not just underneath the house, has their neck bent in an endless servile bow.

A line of identical huts. Just a small step apart, one family in each. The owner built these little homes for his slaves. There's no way out of here. In the rainy season that's literal: the mud is waist-deep. You have to be careful the children don't drown.

Cambodia is trying to catch up with its neighbors, it wants to be an economic tiger, like them. But not at its own expense. You only have to look at who's putting up the tower blocks in

Phnom Penh. Each construction site features a large billboard inscribed with Japanese or Korean, but mainly Chinese characters. Cambodia doesn't have much money, though the politicians' pockets are full. As are those of their wives, husbands, children, and grandchildren. Millions of people in Cambodia have nothing. Just hands to do the work and backs to do the carrying.

We're sitting under the house, in hammocks, and there's a downpour, drumming against the rusted tin. The tipper trucks keep growling away, they're not hindered by the rain as they drive uphill with a load and come back down again, more easily this time; at eye level we can see their large wheels slithering, splashing clay in our faces. It's the afternoon. The slaves are off duty until dawn. To be precise, they start before dawn, at 3 A.M., when it's cooler. They finish at 11 A.M., when the sun and the kilns are so hot that it's unbearable. They work as a trio: Eth, her husband, and their oldest son. He's fifteen, but looks ten. It's been four years since he last went to school. Jointly, they earn seven-and-a-half dollars a day. When there's work. In the rainy season the brick factory has fewer orders, and they do more sitting around.

The middle son? He's nine, he still goes to school at no cost. He's a poor student, he'll stop going soon, like most of the children around here. They can't read or write, just like their parents.

By using a little cunning and wearing a friendly smile you can get inside just about any brick factory with a camera around your neck. And you can see the children, at every factory, running around among the bricks stacked in rows over three hundred feet long. These are the younger children who don't work yet.

They ride bikes along the row of beige kilns, breathing in dust and smoke. The youngest are in their mother's arms or tied to her back while she's stacking bricks. The older kids, aged around twelve, dig up clay, pack it into machines that mold it to form bricks, set the bricks out to dry in the sun, put wood into log-splitting machines, toss the wood into the kilns, load bricks onto wheelbarrows, drive small tractors, and load bricks onto trucks.

There are even smaller children who work, too. We have photographs of them. Child slave labor at the brick factories is also documented by a local organization named LICADHO. In a report on the topic its experts write about some recent accidents: three boys at three brick factories lost their hands. The youngest was seven, the oldest was fourteen. The middle one, aged nine, died from his injuries.

The owners (whom the workers regard as patrons rather than employers, according to the LICADHO report) are never penalized for the children's accidents. Or for their bondage. The police refuse to deal with this widespread crime. There's no prosecutor and no court. The parents are to blame for not supervising their children. Why did he go in among the kilns? Why was he carrying things? It's true, it's the parents who force their children to work because the factory owner pays for each individual brick. The children's labor is worth a lot. If the parents sit quietly, they'll avoid the penalty for a child's accident. The police expect nothing of the brick-factory employees except silence. The police know those people have no money. But the brick-factory owners do. Nobody ever sees how much they pay and to whom. But people are watching during the festivals that last for several days, held at Khmer New Year, or for no particular reason—they see the policemen eating and drinking there on the factory owners' dime.

We wanted to talk to the factory owners, but they're never present. No one at the brick factories knows their phone numbers. That's what they all tell us, always with a smile, of course. So where's the owner's house? Nobody knows. In its report, LICADHO publishes a photo of a grand house. It's an example. The owners live in large houses like this one. The local journalists know their addresses. The ones who work for the English-language newspapers. You can get away with more in English than in Khmer. But only up to a point, because one of the daily papers was closed down recently on the excuse of tax irregularities. There's one more daily paper left. Its reporters sometimes manage to catch the owner of one brick factory or another by the sleeve. They ask about debt bondage. And child labor. What bondage? What debt? What children?

The adults also lose hands, fingers, and eyes at the brick factories. They don't wear protective clothing, gloves, or goggles. The owner pays the hospital bills. Whatever he spends on a worker's treatment is added to their debt. When a brick-factory worker dies, costly ceremonies have to be performed, and the owner's money pays for that too. The dead person's family, his children, have to repay that money. Debt is hereditary.

Debt brings people to the brick factories, and enslaves them for generations. It's quite likely that all the laborers at all the brick factories in Cambodia have taken on this work because of debt. How many brick factories are there in the country? Nobody knows. You see them everywhere—they're located close to the main roads so the trucks can easily drive up, and in the suburbs of the biggest cities: Phnom Penh, Siem Reap, and Sihanoukville. Cities that until recently were three or four stories high now want to reach the clouds. They need bricks, lots of bricks, cheaply, quickly.

People need money. They can give up lots of expenses, but when there's illness in the family, they have to pay. The more serious the illness, the higher the cost. Eth's father had cancer. In Cambodia, children carry their parents' debts throughout their lives. For the life they have received. They're told that over and over again, so they'll never forget: it's thanks to me that you're alive, it's thanks to me that you're on this planet. Paying off a debt of this kind is impossible, but you have to try. So when her father fell ill, Eth borrowed three thousand dollars from a bank. Her father died, but the loan remained. There were no fields in the village, no work. So she went to the brick factory. The patron (as she regards the owner) repaid half of her loan to the bank, and she has to pay back the other half herself. In a good month, she and her husband and son can jointly make more than two hundred dollars.

Seventy-five immediately goes to the bank.

The patron takes another seventy-five for his loan, that's to say two-and-a-half dollars for each day.

How much does that leave out of two hundred?

When a large order comes in, they work in the afternoon as well. Do they earn more? No. Because on those occasions the patron takes more off them. They get the same amount as usual. After the loan payments, they have just enough left for rice.

They buy their rice from the patron. Twenty dollars for fifty kilos. It's more convenient, and cheaper this way.

Water for drinking and for washing also comes from the patron, for a few cents.

Electricity for the lightbulb is from the patron too, free of charge, apparently.

"My youngest son often runs a fever, vomits, and has diarrhea," says Eth. She knows that where children are concerned, it's a short journey from diarrhea to death. Especially in conditions like these. She always goes straight to the doctor. It costs forty dollars for a consultation and medicine. The good patron understands how a mother feels, he sympathizes with her, and never refuses help. Eth is grateful to him. Instead of getting smaller, her debt keeps growing, rapidly, just like a little slave.

Eth has to ask permission to leave before going to the doctor. No problem. But the entire family are never allowed out together. When they go to the lake in the afternoon to look for edible algae, or to gather snails, not everyone can go.

The law in Cambodia forbids slavery. And child labor. There's always a police station somewhere nearby. And the local authorities. And the prime minister's party usually has an office in the neighborhood. There's one in every village. And yet everyone knows about this human bondage, everyone can see the harm that's done to children. Apart from the inspectors—who according to the law should monitor the brick factories regularly. But they don't.

Run away? Where to? The authorities bear responsibility for their citizens' slave labor, the authorities will find the citizen. They'll charge him with stealing money from the brick-factory owner and put him in jail. Or at best send him back to his patron. What will the patron do? Give him a thrashing. Not for free, of course. Because even a beating costs money. His debt will be doubled.

How much does Eth owe the patron now? She spreads her

hands—she doesn't know. The owner has it noted down, the patron keeps count of everything.

The Stump

On every construction site in Phnom Penh, right by the entrance, there has to be a large sign saying: "Safety matters."

To investigate safety, we're traveling to Takeo, on National Highway 2, from Phnom Penh to the south. We're in a shared taxi, five dollars a head. It's a tight squeeze, there's fresh air blowing in; everyone's dressed up, as they always are for a journey, everyone has bathed. Each passenger is careful not to nudge his neighbor, not even to brush an elbow or a knee against him. Foreigners are not to be touched. The people here don't like to touch each other either, and make no gestures, neither publicly, nor at home. Sex is sex, biology. But apart from that, married couples prefer not to come too close. It's the same for parents and children. The further a child can run, the greater the distance. If a child's suffering, you talk, teach, or instruct—you don't hug it. In the past, having emotions got you shot in the head. Or your throat was slit. Are people still afraid to have feelings? Are they still afraid of foreigners? You can talk to a foreigner, you can exchange smiles, it's the right thing to do: where from, where to, with whom, what for? Everyone's curious, everyone wants to discover something about others. The answers don't matter. You don't have to tell a foreigner the truth—why should he want to know the truth? A foreigner knows he's not going to hear the truth. The foreigner also goes by the principle that it doesn't hurt to be cautious when talking to a stranger.

Although the journey only takes two hours, there's an obligatory stop on the way. Both the driver and the passengers are always in agreement that you have to have something to eat en route. Rice, noodles, chicken, meat, chopped-up bones and all; the passengers spit out the bone splinters, and do a lot of talking, but without saying anything. A quick visit to the restroom, and off we go!

We've reached Takeo. A pleasant city, not much trash, some gilded monuments, a few restaurants, a lawn or two, a lake. And a prosthetics factory: four low buildings, a small courtyard shaded by a roof, some wooden benches, and ladders and steps for exercise. There are eleven of these places in Cambodia. The country also boasts a school of prosthetics that's famous throughout the continent. The students are from Afghanistan, Burma, Laos, and Sri Lanka—from places where there are land mines, new or old, and unexploded bombs, from places where there's poverty, from Iraq, North Korea, Georgia, Indonesia, East Timor, Papua New Guinea. And from Cambodia. The prosthetists employed in Takeo make more than one thousand prosthetic limbs each year.

A prosthetic limb: meaning a piece of plastic cast in a mold, fired in a kiln, painted the color of milky coffee, attached to the stump by woven straps, and adjusted to fit using a screwdriver, a saw, and a mallet. Most of them are legs. They don't make many arms here—only if someone's born without one, or if a machine tears off a hand at the brick factory. Men need prostheses twice as often as women. It's roughly the same for children, the young, and the old, though there aren't many old people in Cambodia. Among the new cases, fewer and fewer are land-mine victims, and more and more have been injured in accidents, mostly motorbike crashes. Beer's cheap, the local kind. In these streets, one brewery advertisement faces another. The second is in sight of a third, and the third is looking at a fourth. Most of the ads are red, whatever the brand. You can buy beer anywhere, at any time of day, and there's always a special offer. For every can you buy there's a chance of winning a second beer, sometimes ten dollars, or even a car. If a policeman stops you, you've got to pay him, whether you're drunk or sober.

At the prosthetics factory it's the midday break. We're asked to come back after two. What now? Perhaps we could go to Kraing Ta Chan? Our interpreter, a local English teacher, thinks we should spend some time there.

So we rattle our way to Kraing Ta Chan by tuk-tuk. It's a village amid the rice fields, a short distance from the highway. There's a pagoda in the middle of the village. In the pagoda courtyard there's a tapering stupa, two stories high, glazed on four sides. Behind the glass are five shelves, and on each one there are white skulls. Next to the pagoda there's a farmhouse. The young woman doesn't invite us in, or offer water or tea, as might happen in a similar situation anywhere else in the world. She's not being unfriendly, just cautious of strangers. If they want to sit down, they're welcome to sit down. If there's something they want to know, they're welcome to ask questions.

The billboards? Oh, yes, she's seen them by the village entrance. The drawings on large posters explain what domestic abuse is. A dad with a crazy, menacing face, raising his hand. A mom cringing in terror. The children are crying. People already know it's a bad thing: violence furthers poverty and misery, and violence is punished.

Here? Her cousin used to beat up his wife, everyone heard

the shouting, finally he was killed by a heart attack, and now there's no violence in the village anymore.

The bones? When the cautious woman was little, there were bones sticking out of the ground all over the place. Some still clothed. Under the trees, because the dogs used to bring them from the fields into the shade. The children would go fishing, and the bones would get caught in their nets. "We weren't bothered," she says, "we just threw them back into the water." Until some energetic people appeared, gathered them all up and exhibited them behind glass. The skulls stare at the people who come here to see them. And stare at the people who live here.

"What's that?" ask the village children. "Nothing. Just bones," their parents reply. "Just bones," say their grandparents, as if they saw nothing and remember nothing. Are the children frightened by the bones? Do they ever see ghosts? Of course not! Ghosts come out at night, when the children are asleep. In the daytime either the rain's falling, or the sun is shining, the rice is growing, the cats are idling, the dogs are barking, the skulls are staring, and the children are playing with a Chinese jump rope.

"I never asked what they did with my bones," says Chum Sokchea, aged thirty-four, tall, thin, and gloomy. We've gone back to Takeo, to the prosthetics factory, for our meeting. What does he have to be cheerful about? He's hobbling on a crutch that looks like a spade handle. He tucks it under his armpit and gets going. He's not finding it easy. He's waiting for a new leg and will stay here for a while—there are rooms for patients in one of the factory buildings. The patients don't have to pay, a notice stuck to the wall informs us. We already know that this is an exception. Everywhere else in the local health service, the patients pay for everything. But here, Sokchea is also getting a dollar-and-a-half a day, so he won't go hungry.

"At the construction site I was earning five dollars a day," he starts to tell us what happened. Not once does he look us in the eyes. He was working in Phnom Penh, where these days something's being built on every street. The city is rising upward, getting richer. Sokchea was building apartments. The well-to-do like to live high up, looking down on the poor from above. The poor work in flip-flops. Sokchea used to pump water, carry things, clean, and paint—he didn't know how to do anything else. He slept in a tent with five other men. He doesn't know how many tents there were, but around seventy laborers spent the night there, men, women, on the eleventh floor, on the sixteenth, on the third, they pitched those tents on the concrete in the future bedrooms, guest rooms, children's rooms, kitchens, and bathrooms. But in reception halls, bars, casinos, gyms, and swimming pools too, because in his career as a laborer Sokchea built high-rise hotels as well. Every day, seven days a week, he started at seven in the morning and worked until eleven. Then again from one in the afternoon until five. "In other words, it was a decent job," he tells us, "eight hours, five dollars, the boss paid us reliably. Over three years we kept changing construction sites, but not once was he ever late with the pay."

Until *that* day came. Sokchea was painting a wall, standing on scaffolding that started to wobble; he fell off it, and couldn't get up. He was taken to the hospital. His boss paid for that as well, without dispute, though not every employer pays the medical bills when there's an accident. Accidents on construction sites are a daily occurrence. The doctors said the bones in his right leg were shattered; they found a way to splint the leg, and gave him some pills for the pain. He was all alone at the hospital, with no family care; he left after two days and rested for several weeks. Once he thought the bones had knitted together, he went back to the construction site. He pumped water, carried, and cleaned, always in flip-flops. The pain came back again, intensifying from one month to the next, but Sokchea was brave, a year flew by, and then the leg began to suppurate. He went home. He had no employment contract and no insurance. His wife? She took their child and left. What use to her was a husband who couldn't earn a living? He hasn't seen his daughter for two years now. Throughout that time he's been in and out of the hospital. The doctors told him his bones were in pieces, and that instead of growing together they were rotting. No one ever supported him at the hospital, no one brought him food or helped him to use the toilet. He requested an amputation, and they performed it. Three months have gone by since he lost his right leg. He asked to be discharged, and they discharged him. They wheeled him to a taxi. The taxi driver asked him about the future. Sokchea would have been happy to share some profound thoughts with the taxi driver, but his mind was as empty as a slum when the paupers have been evicted. He went to his mother's house. She opened the door, took one look at his stump and said: "I'd rather you were dead."

Four Bald Death's-Heads

We're driving back from Takeo to Phnom Penh along National Highway 2.

Around twenty miles outside the capital we turn left, onto a new, smooth stretch of asphalt that leads to the zoo. Two miles further on, the road ends at a quiet temple and a barrier. Behind a fence is a crocodile in a swampy pool, some bears rescued from slavery, and a tiger in a pen, an animal that's locally been wiped out in the wild. It's the usual suffering of captive creatures, there's nothing more to be seen here. Nor is there any respite for the eye on this side of the barrier, no houses along the surfaced road, just dry bushes left and right. There's no shade.

The women look like bushes too. At first they're hard to spot, they're the colors of the earth, sand, and air. They're squatting singly at the side of the road, one every three hundred, or six hundred feet. The cars zoom by—out in the sticks the drivers like to step on the gas, but each woman jumps out under the wheels suddenly, like a startled deer that doesn't realize it'll be killed by the impact. Each one hurls herself at the bumper with the energy of a missile, with her hands raised and her mouth open in a shout. But there's no shout to be heard. Don't they have the strength to shout? As if using the last of their energy, as if they weren't afraid of death. Like skin-coated skeletons, monsters, they lie across the car hoods, shaved almost bald, bent double, fiercely determined. Each one's holding a stick. Every day the sun blazes down mercilessly in this sandy wilderness. They're hungry.

Now they're all hurrying toward us, because we've stopped beside the first one. And we're not driving away. It's probably a rare event, ever since they laid the asphalt two years ago. Before then, a muddy road ran down here from the national highway. The rich people's cars used to rumble slowly over the potholes. Even if there weren't many of them on this stretch of road, it was easy to grab hold of a handle and open a door, best of all a rear one—the children would instantly start to cry. They'd come here to see a tiger in a cage, but instead they were met by a toothless

old hag, evidently doing her best to join the family inside the
car, at which the mother and father would immediately toss her
a small banknote, just to get rid of her. Now the practice has
become more difficult, because the asphalt's smooth, the cars
race by, and a person grows older, not younger.

"The old have to eat too," says the first one, by whom
we've stopped. She's been on duty here every morning for ten
years. She's eighty, and has nothing. She's dressed in rags, but
is clean. All her life she wove mats, until finally her eyes and
fingers refused to do the job. Three daughters, two sons, lots
of grandchildren—around twenty of them. She lives with her
daughter and son-in-law, a couple of miles from here; they sell
water and soft drinks outside their house, that's how they make
their living. Every morning, her fifteen-year-old grandson brings
her here by scooter to do her begging, and leaves her hungry.
She's always hungry: in the morning, there's congee, as thin as
it was in Pol Pot's day, at noon a handful of boiled rice in the
bundle she's brought with her. Sometimes with the rice she has
two little dried fish the size of a child's finger. And so it goes until
evening. Before sundown, her grandson comes to fetch her. Her
daughter takes away the dollar she has earned by begging. She
doesn't always succeed in earning a dollar, and on those days the
family refuses her a bowl of rice soup in the evening.

"You've got a good life," the second woman says to that; she's
over eighty too, and also poorly but cleanly dressed. "At least
nobody beats you. And you don't have to watch your daughter
being beaten every day. My son-in-law? Endlessly drunk,
endlessly dissatisfied with us. My daughter can't give me a single
grain of rice, because he's got his eye on us, just like the black
shirts. Keeping us in check is the only thing he's capable of—he

does nothing else. At least he lets my grandchildren talk to me, but they don't have any sympathy for me either. They can't give me anything. I don't give them anything either. I'm of no use, I'm nobody's, ever since my husband died, in Pol Pot's day. I got married a long time ago, before my sixteenth birthday, and we had eight children. Pol Pot starved seven of them to death. The oldest was named Chum. The second was Kun. The third was Chin. The fourth was Oun. The fifth . . . what was the fifth one called? Poverty's addling my wits, or it could be old age. I can't remember my own children. The sixth? The seventh? I can't remember their names or faces. Oh yes—there's still Nhet! Her husband beats her, did I tell you that already?"

"I was beaten too," says the first woman. "In Pol Pot's day, my husband . . ."

At this point a third beggar woman, the same age as the others, interrupts her. "Who knows what's better?" she says. "I never had a husband or children. I've been nobody's from the day I learned to walk. I've always been an orphan. We're a land of orphans, there was so much killing here. All I have is an older brother who's been lying flat for years, slowly dying for years. We live with his widowed daughter. Her husband never did a thing except play cards. And drink. Finally he went off into the world. He's alive. Did I say he was dead? No, she's not a widow. We just say that, otherwise people would gossip and say she left her husband, they'd say she's a whore. What's my name? For as long as I can remember nobody has ever asked me my name."

"It's as if old women don't have names," adds the second, the one who can't remember her own children. "No one ever calls us by name. We're all called Granny. By our own families, and by strangers. 'Go to the road, Granny! Make yourself useful, Granny! Fuck off, Granny!'"

The youngest of the women squatting by the road joins us. She's not yet sixty, but she looks like the oldest. Her right hand and right foot never stop shaking. Her mother was in a motorbike accident while she was pregnant with her; as a result her daughter was born with a damaged hip, and limps to this day. But that's not why she shakes on her right side. That's from her marriage. Even when she gave birth to her daughter, her husband never stopped beating her. He hit her hard. Always on the head first. She left him too late, too late. In fact, it was he who left her, too late. For a younger woman. Now he torments the younger woman. Luckily it's not her problem anymore. Her daughter didn't have a good childhood. Now her daughter has high blood pressure, a cross-eyed child of her own, and a husband who beats her. "I live in a shack next to my daughter," says the youngest beggar. "I can hear everything through the boards. My son-in-law's every curse, his every blow, and every cry of pain made by my daughter. There's water inside my hut instead of a floor, but it doesn't matter, I hang my hammock between the walls. I can reach out and touch both walls. I bang my head on the ceiling."

The Magic Boy
The boy's name is Kong Keng; he's two years old, and he lives in a wooden house on pillars. The lame, blind, deaf, and ulcerated made pilgrimages to visit him from all over the country. They came alone, or they were carried here by their relatives. Sometimes it took several days. "Will sick people start coming

here from abroad?" asked the local newspapers, "in wheelchairs and on stretchers, now that the press in Vietnam, Laos, and Thailand has written about the Khmer child's miraculous powers? There's even been a report in the English-language daily, *The Bangkok Post*, which is read worldwide by those interested in South-East Asian affairs."

For the healing touch of his little hands, or rather—as the local radio stations kept saying—for a blessing from the Magic Boy, each desperate wretch had to pay a dollar. Gifts were also welcomed, such as a can of Red Bull or a packet of cigarettes for the boy's grandfather.

The newspapers reported that the grandfather had been in extremely poor health. He wasn't at all well, but with the last of his strength he'd taken his grandson in his arms; perhaps he thought his final hour had come, or maybe he wanted the scent of a loved one to accompany him on his journey into the afterlife— the journalists didn't explain this point, but in any case, they stated clearly that his grandson's touch had suddenly cured him.

Once the boy's mysterious abilities had come to light, a pretty good harvest was soon flowing into the village, a rapid stream of cash, a magical gold mine. For many weeks the relatives collected the money in plastic bowls. And they had plenty to collect, because up to a thousand people waited in line each day. Worn out, weak, and sweaty, they lay on dusty mats, groaning, as the heat blazed down; their healthy relatives picked up banana leaves to fan them with, and they all grew hungry and thirsty. So the local residents didn't waste the opportunity, as we can see on YouTube: they cooked rice, various kinds of soup, and green vegetables, they served duck eggs and coconut milk, and were soon doing roaring trade, amid the atmosphere of a fair, or a fiesta, with music, pipes and drums, plenty of Chinese crap on sale, including cheap, brightly colored toys—it was worth buying any old thing as a gift for the little miracle worker, as then one's chances of being cured were vastly multiplied.

After a while, the little kru khmer was tired of all the toys, the clamor, and the moist stranger's hands from dawn to dusk. He was annoyed, and began to protest. The whole house was shaking, and every day the crowd of ailing people thickened, pressing forward as if half the country had come here. Most were Khmer peasants: skin tanned by the sun, weary eyes, bones protruding, old clothes, old slip-ons. Were they all hoping for good health? Did they all want a long life?

The loving mother, Mrs. Phat Soeun, aged twenty-one, took her son away to the home of relatives nearby. An announcement was made: from now on, the Magic Boy would only treat the most difficult cases. Those who weren't granted access to him wouldn't go away with nothing. They too would be healed. They would simply have to buy some sticks of magic incense, a dollar each. Or some magic green leaves. Or a bottle of eucalyptus balsam, each one touched by the little healer. Because, naturally, everything on sale had been blessed by the Magic Boy. Smoke from the incense was to be breathed in slowly, and the leaves were to be added to tea for several days. According to *The Bangkok Post*, five hundred to seven hundred of the aromatic packets were sold each day. The village chief, Mr. Sou Hen, used his authority to testify that the medicines work extremely well—the blind can see, the paralyzed can walk.

But the journalists couldn't find anyone who'd been healed. So they asked the people waiting in line why they were letting themselves be duped. The sick and their relatives refused to listen to such nasty questions. Doctors? They're expensive—all over Cambodia we hear the same mantra, the doctors are far away, the doctors couldn't help, so they came here.

And then they left. There's been no crowd of sick people here for quite a time, as we know from the newspapers. The Magic Boy stopped healing. There's nothing special going on outside his home anymore.

We decided to go and see the boy.

People point to the east. A long way! The closer we get to the Vietnamese border, the more often we have to stop, open the window and ask. Everyone knows where he did his healing, so they show us the way with a smile. Finally, we drive off the highway, go another half mile or so down a dirt road, and reach Khnor.

The healer's house? It's here! There's a gray-haired woman standing in front of us, with a little boy in her arms. It's him, asleep, sullen, not interested in visitors. His grandmother, Mrs. Torm Hut, aged sixty, invites us inside. We go up a wide ladder. One room, no furniture, with a latticed bamboo floor. Without being asked, the lady of the house explains by way of introduction that the family only built themselves a walled toilet with running water, which stands behind the house. The rest of the money was taken to the nearest temple.

It was the monks who must have been worried when the little Kong Keng stopped healing. He grew out of his miraculous powers, explains his grandmother, and the people vanished. The family lives modestly, as before. The boy's parents work a long way off, somewhere on a farm, which is why they're not at home; they each earn five dollars a day there, and they come home once every few weeks. What about the grandfather? He comes to join us. His name is Sen Ban, and he's over sixty, but it wasn't him the miracle boy cured, it was his uncle. The grandfather laughs at us for quoting these media inaccuracies, and hugs his grandson, as grandfathers hug their grandsons the world over. The photographer holds up his camera and asks if he can take a picture. Meanwhile the neighbors, male and female, have also climbed up to join us, all friendly and talkative: Khnor is less than half a mile square, there's not much land, not much rice, 250 families, and seventeen hundred souls. Including a smiling man who joins us an hour later, and tells us in a quiet voice that his name is Ou Seng; he's ninety-nine, and is the Magic Boy's great-grandfather.

It's unusual to meet someone as old as Ou Seng in Cambodia. There aren't many people twenty-five years younger than he is here. Why not? It would be worth asking the ancient great-grandfather about that, but conversation tires him. He doesn't say much. But he remembers everything: the French, and the Japanese, and King Sihanouk, the Vietnamese from the north, the Vietnamese from the south, the Americans, General Lon Nol, Pol Pot and the Khmer Rouge, and Hun Sen, who's still in power today. No one and nothing has broken the great-grandfather: no persecutions, no bombings, no war, no slave labor, no illness, and no famine—"You may take my picture, young man."

The Village Doctor
We've headed north-west, toward the Thai border, in the direction of Battambang. Several hours exposed to the blare of car horns, exhaust fumes, and strong sunlight. There are stone houses standing close together on either side of the road— evidently their owners worked for Thais. And others plainly

didn't, because most of the dwellings here are sheds cobbled together from straw and boards with holes in them. There are some flat, green spaces—for the local paupers they're a source of food, including fruit, vegetables, and rice. What else apart from rice? Someone has acquired a cow, someone else has not. Someone has hens, someone else has not. The local people used to eat snakes, and sold the skins across the Thai border, until they went too far with the reptile trade. The snakes disappeared, which is why there are so many rats now. And people eat the rats. We too can buy ourselves skewered rat from a roadside barbecue.

We're going to a village named Roka. Things have been bad there for some time, the negative statistics have been rising, the newspapers have been writing about them, a hundred people have already been affected by dramatic events, two hundred, almost three, whole families are living in fear, the authorities have been making announcements and promising to sort out the problem. But how? The damage cannot be undone.

One third of the inhabitants of Roka cannot read or write, as we already know, so nothing here can surprise us. We ask the authorities in Battambang, the provincial capital, when they first realized what was happening. Dr. Voeurng Bunreth, director of the health department, explains: teams of hygienists went from village to village, taking blood samples from randomly selected people. HIV screening is carried out all over Cambodia. Of eleven people tested in the village of Roka, three turned out to be HIV positive: two adults and a child. That's too many. The next day, thirty of the villagers were asked to give blood. The results indicated a dozen more HIV-positive villagers. Then more people were tested—the number of HIV-positive cases reached one hundred, then two hundred, then more. Those infected included old men and women—who in the view of the authorities were no longer sexually active—and children whose mothers had negative results, meaning the children hadn't been infected in the womb, or through their mothers' milk, but in some other way. Half of those with a positive diagnosis were also found to be carrying hepatitis C.

Roka is a collection of shabby houses scattered within a quiet grove. There's a large, brick temple, and a one-story health center with two consulting rooms. No doctor has ever worked here. So when the local people fell sick, they went to see a neighbor, next to the clinic. He was an "unauthorized doctor"—the authorities know about him by now, and so does the press. But the authorities have promised to combat illegal medical practices, and they're always making beguiling announcements. It'll be interesting to see if they succeed. What will they provide to residents instead?

Anyone without money could get an injection from their neighbor on credit. The press gives this nice "doctor's" first and family name, and says that he liked to treat people with injections. He'd use the same needle until it grew blunt or broke. Now he's in prison, accused of mass murder, and facing a life sentence.

The doctor—in the village they still call him the doctor—was capable of giving one person up to thirty injections in the course of a few consultations. The locals are willing to talk about it. We don't ask anyone about their test results. They tell us of their own accord who has the virus and who doesn't. It's no secret. They gave blood together, and got the results together. A negative result wasn't communicated behind the door of a consulting room—who'd have thought of preserving confidentiality? Who'd have expected it of the authorities? Everyone knows all about everyone else.

A woman points to her elderly mother and one of her own children—they've got it. But her other child, injected again and again, doesn't. And her husband was injected too, but is negative. Now he's working far away, on someone's farm, and only comes home once a month. She's carrying the anxiety alone. So what if the drugs are free of charge? They don't treat minds and souls. Yet the virus is also an illness of the soul. A form of isolation. The sufferer feels inferior, rejected, afraid, and doesn't know what to do next. Nobody is explaining anything to anyone. And nobody is providing anything to eat. Medication isn't food.

The director of the health department is particularly concerned about how some of the infected people eat a poor diet. Almost all of them are suffering from depression. But there are only two psychiatrists at work in the entire province. Stress and poor nutrition don't help the treatment. If only the infected people ate well, took their medication, and had less stress, they could live to an old age. They won't.

Three years have gone by since it all started. The total numbers: 296 infected, thirty dead. The sentence for the "doctor": twenty-five years in jail.

The Bookseller

Outside the gates of the provincial hospital in Siem Reap, a man named Teng Dara works on Pub Street. He hasn't been to see a doctor for almost a quarter of a century. He's a bookseller. Most of the books he sells are in English, with a few in French, possibly a couple in German, but none in Khmer. They're all about the last few decades: about the French, who finally left, about King Sihanouk, about General Lon Nol, about the American air raids, about the genocide. And about the black shadow the bloodshed of that era still casts on everyday life in Cambodia.

Teng Dara could tell the tourists plenty of things himself. Someone should ask him a few questions. About who he is, for instance. But people only ever ask him the prices of the books, nothing more, and just smile. They're not interested in the fact that when the bookseller was a child the Viet Cong invaded his village near the border, then the Vietnamese from the south invaded it, or maybe it was the other way around, chronology isn't his strong point; there were arrests, accusations of collaboration with the enemy, the men were massacred, and the women were raped. There are still no books about the mass rape. Sexual violence under the Khmer Rouge is still a suppressed topic. In his village, the majority lived within stone walls, and worked for General Lon Nol, and for the king before that, whereas the neighboring villages, the ones in the jungle, with no roads or stone walls, with no windows, just wood, clay and straw, supported Pol Pot. Who would want to hear about such events on Pub Street nowadays? Who would be able to take it all in, over a pint of Angkor beer? Anyway, eventually the men in black shirts arrived, known to the world as the Khmer Rouge (though King Sihanouk was the first to call them that), and killed off just about everyone because the Khmer Rouge didn't like surfaced roads, they didn't like stone houses, and they didn't like windows.

And he could talk about *that* day. That day came when Dara was twenty-four years old, and had been serving in Hun Sen's army for seven. That name is still important in Cambodia today. It's the most important name of all.

In those days, Hun Sen was the prime minister, and he's the prime minister now as well. But once, a long time ago, he was in the Khmer Rouge, then he escaped to Vietnam, and returned to Cambodia with the Vietnamese. For almost thirty years Hun Sen has been the head of government. By will of the sovereign, naturally.

Teng Dara is now over fifty. On that day in 1990, he was walking along with a fellow soldier, who was also twenty-four at the time; they were chatting, and didn't notice the wire stretched at a height of four inches between a tree and an anti-personnel mine. The Soviet-made mine, shaped like a corn cob, and laid by their own troops, was meant to be a trap for Pol Pot's men, who were still roaming the jungle here and there. The explosion tore off one of his comrade's legs. It tore off both of Dara's, ripped through his intestines, and mutilated an eye. These days he sees the world through just one.

He starts work each day before 10 A.M., and has to get out of here before seven in the evening. At dusk, Pub Street, where Dara usually wheels his bookstore from one restaurant to the next, becomes a noisy crush, and no wonder—each year, let's remember, two-and-a-half million tourists visit the nearby Angkor temples. They fly here from every continent, almost all of them stay overnight in the vicinity, and they drink beer on this plasticky street lit in red, or on the equally red-lit neighboring streets. In this global tumult, nobody would be interested in buying non-fiction from Dara. And in such a chaotic crowd it'd be hard to maneuver his bicycle-cart full of books, driven by the power of his arms.

He only works during the day, sometimes managing to sell three books, sometimes ten. Always too few. But he has plenty of expenses. He doesn't look after himself, though he should—for some time he's been bothered by stomach pains and a blood-flecked cough. But Dara gave up on doctors long ago, and can't remember when he last went to see one. Probably when he was returning to life after the mine blew up.

And he did return. He has children, and he works to provide for them. His youngest son is two years old, and often accompanies his father. Or his mother, who also sells books from a second cart. Dara's wife is named Malay, she has both legs and she's thirty. They'd like to sell sunglasses from their carts because they're more popular with the tourists, but they're much more expensive than books, and can cost up to thirty-five dollars. For now there's no question of it—Dara doesn't have the money for merchandise of that kind. Dara and Malay's older son is seven, but he lives far away with his grandmother, in another province. Dara's mother, on her own and in poor health, needs care, so they sent her grandson to live with her. He brings her water, and nips out to the store, but because of the separation from his parents he's not getting enough education, and he often runs a fever. Once a month Dara has to send them thirty dollars. And he does it with difficulty.

He works hard. Better to work than to beg. Those who've had the misfortune to be blown up by a mine with only partial success, as Dara puts it, usually end up wiping the curb with their bodies, drunk on the cheapest booze. That sort of life doesn't last long. Dara almost ended up that way, but then he had himself smuggled into Thailand. Begging is more fruitful there. Eight times the Thai police arrested him, eight times he was deported, and eight times he went back. It was worth it. In Thailand he saw what he hadn't seen in Cambodia: everyone works without exception, including people like him. He could even tell the story of how he acquired his first, then his second, and then his third bicycle-cart, this wonderful, shabby bookstore on wheels, which he propels manually.

The Man Who Photographed the Moment Before the End

His story starts in an ordinary way: "I was born on September 9, 1961, in the village of Trapaing Meas in Kampong Chhnang province. My mom died when I was two years old. I finished fourth grade at junior school, then for twenty-five years I had no education at all. There were eight of us brothers; five are no longer alive. Eventually I went back to school, and graduated from high school and university. I have a wife and seven children. Six, actually, because one of ours has already died."

He tells his story with detail and self-confidence. It just worked out that way, it's not his fault, it wasn't his choice, what could he do, he wanted to live.

He has no doubts: "They didn't know why I was taking their picture."

"The prison photographer's name is known—Nhem Ein—and can be cited," writes Susan Sontag in her book-length essay, *Regarding the Pain of Others.* "These Cambodian women and men of all ages, including many children, photographed from a few feet away, usually in half figure, are—as in Titian's *The Flaying of Marsyas,* where Apollo's knife is eternally about to descend—forever looking at death, forever about to be murdered, forever wronged. And the viewer is in the same position as the lackey behind the camera; the experience is sickening."

Phnom Penh in April 1975: the first arrests, the first prisons, the first torture and executions. Members of the previous, pro-American regime, against whom the Khmer Rouge had been fighting for five years, were the first to be liquidated: politicians, civil servants, military personnel from General Lon Nol's army, and some members of the royal family. And intellectuals: every one of them had served the traitors. Doctors, engineers, teachers, and artists would be unnecessary to the new society.

Schools were closed, banks were destroyed, money was abolished, cars were banned. None of it was ever going to be needed again. The old names of the Khmer provinces were done away with, and were instead given numbers. A new calendar was announced, starting from Year Zero.

The secret S-21 prison was soon up and running, at Tuol Sleng high school in the south of Phnom Penh. It consists of several three-story blocks within an enclosed, leafy campus. Each building had a stairwell on either side. They were linked by long balconies, forming the front elevation—open galleries that led into the classrooms.

Today we're going inside up the same stairs. Today we're walking through all those rooms, a crowd of us. We've come from Poland, Australia, France, Martinique, Italy, Taiwan, Venezuela, Great Britain, and Switzerland. And we're looking at a metal bed. It's the only object in this ground-floor room, in the building to the left of the gate. A rather rusty exhibit, between yellow, stained walls, on cold terracotta that was once wet with blood. The torturers would chain the person to the bed and start their interrogation. Now we're inspecting the torturer's tools: pincers, shackles, collars, and chains. Somewhere alongside lie clothes and hats. Outside are some gallows for near-choking and some large vats for near-drowning.

There are cells in the next building over. The classrooms were divided by wooden or brick partitions. Dozens of cramped, gloomy boxes, half without windows. You used to be able to hear the prisoners howling here at night. Now we're peering into these burrows. One cell after another. The doors weren't necessary. The "guilty" person, and every prisoner was that, was chained by the foot to a metal hook sunk into the concrete. There was a bucket in each cell, the guides are telling us. Or not telling us, if we chose to tour in silence. Many of us prefer silence, and we walk through the Genocide Museum singly, in solitude.

Photographs. Portraits shortly before death. Black and white. One beside another. Face after face. The eyes. In glass display cases. In rows—you could count them by the yard. Some of them repeat. Exhibits. Hundreds of pictures from the six thousand negatives found here by the Vietnamese soldiers, who captured Phnom Penh in January 1979 after four years of Pol Pot's dictatorship, and ousted him. These are not all of the people who were photographed at S-21. According to the sources, there were at least fourteen thousand victims of the secret prison. And they stress: there were undoubtedly far more. Maybe twice as many, perhaps even more than that.

The S-21 prison was established for "counter-revolutionaries" and "spies." For those who had previously swelled the ranks of the Khmer Rouge. Most of them were young men from the countryside. And a few older ones, who had already managed to perform some function within the communist apparatus, at the central or local level. The "enemies" were brought here in trucks from all over the country.

Members of the former regime who hadn't already been killed also ended up here. And some foreigners—fools who dared to stay in the country when it was time to get out.

The "enemy" was usually arrested along with their relatives, neighbors, and friends. Whole families ended up here, including small children. Now we can see them in the photos. We certainly won't forget their eyes for a long time: vacant, empty, mindless, resigned, suspended, in anticipation, as if glued to the wall of the dentist's waiting room, unstuck from reality. Or else they're aware of everything, proud, determined, full of indignation, astonishment, distaste, fury, panic, horror. Almost every face has a number.

The prisoners who don't have numbers weren't taken to the cells after having their picture taken. They weren't interrogated. They were herded back onto the trucks and taken to the killing fields outside the city. Now they're here, looking at us from their photographs.

On the other side of the narrow street, opposite the gates of Tuol Sleng, stands a shabby stall. It hardly attracts anyone's attention. The tuk-tuk drivers call out to the crowd of people emerging from the museum. They'll take them to the city center for two or three dollars. For beer, for wine, for good Khmer food. At the stall is a young woman trying to sell a book for ten dollars apiece. She has several copies. Newly published. The cover shows some of the small photographs already familiar to us from the museum. One picture is larger than the rest: of a boy in a cap. That's how the author looked as a teenager. His unassuming little book, or rather booklet, is an amateur publication. The text and pictures are printed on coated paper. It's a concise account in English. In Cambodia, books about Cambodia are not published in the Khmer language, and if they are, they're rare. The truth about the genocide, about everything that preceded it and that happened after it, is an export product—for foreign visitors. For the locals, a chapter in the school textbook is enough. You can write more in English than in Khmer. Or so it seemed to everyone here until recently. There were two daily English-language newspapers in Phnom Penh that wrote bolder articles: not just about the genocide, but also about today's poverty, and human rights abuse, about corruption, nepotism, and the kleptocracy. Recently, let us repeat, the authorities put one of the dailies up against the wall on the pretext of tax irregularities. It stopped appearing. The other one is still in print. For how much longer? Because there's nowhere in the local media to call the ruling politicians to account. And it's still too soon for a reckoning with recent history. Under international pressure, a tribunal has in fact started to operate in Phnom Penh, with the task of trying the leaders of the Khmer Rouge. Only the leaders—that's what Cambodia agreed with the world. The authorities washed the blood from the hands of the rank-and-file assassins by a special legal act issued in 1995. This law also applied to the man who photographed the victims of S-21 prison.

The tribunal (part international, part Cambodian) has to hurry: the leaders of the genocide are old, and they're slipping away from the human world. At first the ordinary Khmers closely followed the tribunal hearings. They wanted justice. But they didn't understand much of what was going on in the courtroom. There aren't many journalists here who can explain to viewers and readers what it's all about. There are no public debates, especially on such difficult topics. And the work of the prosecutors and judges has been dragging on, the local media are increasingly reluctant to cover them, in ever shorter reports. Genocide doesn't attract advertisers. And the readers are fed up with the tribunal, or rather disappointed by it. Over ten years have passed since the first acts of indictment, but only a few people have been convicted. For exterminating a million citizens? Millions of dollars have been spent on this legal process, and more money all the time. What for? Wouldn't it be better spent on building a clinic in the countryside? A hospital? Or a road? People don't have the strength for justice anymore. They don't want to read about the genocide. So nobody takes any notice of the book, published in English and sold at a stall outside the Tuol Sleng Genocide Museum. The title is *The Khmer Rouge's Photographer at S-21*. The author is Nhem Ein.

The name of a second author appears on the cover in small print. This must be the person who wrote out the S-21 photographer's words in simple English. He also added a short introduction. In a greatly abridged form it says: "I am convinced the fascinating story of Nhem Ein should be told. He is the only photographer from S-21 to have survived a long journey with the Khmer Rouge. He is a key witness to our genocide. Everyone knows that Democratic Kampuchea, the Khmer Rouge, or Angkar, in other words the Supreme Organization, brought us nothing but devastation. And that those who survived can be regarded as fortunate. But can they really? We all lost loved ones. None of us has forgotten the forced labor for Angkar: the long hours without a break, the starvation diet, and the torture. Communicating with one's own children was forbidden. Asking questions was prohibited. The only things allowed were obedience, or death.

The Khmer Rouge killed entire families. Their dictatorship left me and all the other survivors with the most dreadful memories. Mental and physical pain to this day. Each of us is affected by death.

"To this day, most of us cannot understand why the Khmer Rouge killed so many people. What were they trying to achieve?

"Only seven victims survived S-21 prison.

"And Nhem Ein. The victims' photographer.

"As co-author of his book, I dedicate my work to the memory of my father, who was killed by the Khmer Rouge. I was three years old at the time. And to the memory of my aunt, my uncle, my grandparents, and all the other victims. Signed in Phnom Penh on November 20, 2014, Dara Duong, child survivor of the killing fields."

On the very first page there's a phone number for the victims' photographer. Nobody picks up. So for now let's take a look at what he writes about.

He was thirteen when the Khmer Rouge "liberated" Phnom Penh. But he had belonged to the Organization since early childhood. In April, 1975, it had sent him to the capital. He had never been there before. He'd walked along roads ravaged by the war, against the tide, because long columns of barefooted people were trailing in the opposite direction. He felt excitement and trepidation. He reached the city. To him it looked beautiful. He was quartered along with two thousand other teenagers—they too had been taken away from their families. He felt pride. He was told to study tactical and technical skills useful on the battlefield. Democratic Kampuchea needed soldiers. The children were divided into groups. The groups were given serious designations: the air force, the navy, the land forces, and military strategy. They were examined to see which children were the most intelligent, who carried out orders and obeyed the rules. And the rules concerned sleeping, eating, walking, sitting, speaking, showing emotion, dressing, tidiness, and hygiene. The children who didn't measure up to the expectations were sent to the rice fields or to front-line units on the Vietnamese border. The more disciplined ones were sent to a clothes factory in the city.

One hundred and forty-one bright and healthy teenagers were selected. The best Children of Angkar. They were sent to China for training. Among them was the author of the book we're now reading. The future victims' photographer.

He's still not answering his phone.

Further on he writes how:

+ Before leaving for China he worked as a courier. He delivered letters addressed in red ink, always to a specific individual. By bicycle, from the hospital in the city of Ta Kmao to the Monivong hospital in Phnom Penh. And back again. Nobody ever guessed the courier was a boy. Because in accordance with the battlefield tactic he'd been taught, he covered his face with a scarf and spoke in a high-pitched voice. There were other secret prisons in operation next to the hospitals. The letters contained orders—whom to interrogate and whom to execute.

+ Before his departure for China his entire family was vetted. They were all found to be in order, and had supported the Khmer Rouge since at least 1970.

+ The Children of Angkar sailed to China in early 1976 by ship from the port at Sihanoukville. The voyage took a week. To avoid sea sickness, twice a day they were allowed to come on deck to breathe some fresh air and look at the waves.

+ The children were trained by Chinese people, with the help of Khmer translators. Once a month, Comrade Son Sen came to see them in person. He was one of the Khmer Rouge leaders, murdered many years later, most likely by Pol Pot. The training involved various military topics. Each child was observed. They noticed that fourteen-year-old Nhem Ein was bright and exceptionally disciplined. And he alone was singled out to attain some special skills—mapping and photography. For the next six months he was taught how to draw maps, how to do landscape photography, and how to photograph portraits.

+ He returned to Cambodia with the same group of children, on the same ship. All the former trainees were sent to do various tasks within the army. He was sent to S-21 prison in Tuol Sleng school.

The photographer finally answers his phone. He's busy, he apologizes, and asks us to call back in an hour. In the course of an hour, we can read his thin book twice and make our preparations for a conversation with him. He wasn't yet fifteen, he was terrified, but he quickly realized he couldn't show any emotion. No feelings in front of the guards or the prison commander, Comrade Duch—recently sentenced by the tribunal to thirty years in prison, extended after a failed appeal to life. The photographer testified before the high court, where he said roughly what he has written in the book. Only obeying the rules and carrying out his orders could save him from death. The orders were clear: to take photographs. Five other photographers worked with him. None of them are alive anymore. The author lists their names, but he doesn't say when and in what circumstances they died.

They were all given the same uniforms. Black ones. Three sets a year. And a uniform from China, for special occasions. Sometimes they were given extra items, including two undershirts, two scarves, and three pairs of underpants. Sandals made of cut-up tires. Anyone who owned more than that was penalized.

They were given a dozen cameras and the necessary equipment for developing the photos. They started taking pictures at 7 A.M., because the "guilty" were often brought in at dawn. They had lunch at noon. They went back to work at two, and finished at five. Then they had other duties: growing vegetables in the prison garden, feeding the hens and rabbits. If a truck full of the "guilty" arrived in the evening, they had to drop everything and stand behind their cameras.

The kitchen could make meals for four hundred people. Comrade Duch ate here with his staff. The prisoners were given watery rice gruel. Enough to keep them from dying of hunger before the interrogations ended. The people who worked here were well provided for. There was poultry, fish, bread, and desserts. For four years the photographer was unaware that outside the prison, large numbers of Khmers were dying of starvation. That was because he didn't get into lengthy conversations with the people who were brought to S-21. He didn't ask them any questions. If they asked him a question, he kept quiet.

They were brought before the camera straight from the trucks. With their hands tied behind their backs—that's plain to see in the photos—and blindfolded. The guards would remove the blindfolds, and the photographer helped.

Some "enemies" had bruised, blood-stained faces. They'd been beaten up in transit.

If they were terrified, the photographer asked them to make an effort to calm down.

To take a seat on the chair.

Comfortably.

The chair had a head rest. We can see it today in the museum.

The photographer asked them to keep still for a moment.

And to be quiet.

To look at the lens.

Without blinking.

He was careful, because each photo had to come out perfect, and there was no chance of correcting it. Even the slightest screw-up, or so he assures us in the book, could have meant the end of him. Many of the guards who'd tortured people at the prison also ended up in the killing fields later on, because somehow or other they'd brought shame on the commander. The same thing happened to an entire group of cooks who hadn't made the soup on time. Comrade Duch was cruel, Comrade Duch was unforgiving. So even when the guards were hurrying the photographer along, even when the "guilty" were waiting in a long line, he had to work carefully. Both in the room that was the studio, and afterward, in the darkroom.

Some prisoners were interrogated for several days, others for many weeks. The faster the torture victim gave all the names of the "spies" collaborating with him, the quicker he admitted to having contacts within the CIA, the KGB, or Vietnamese intelligence, the sooner he ended up on the truck. That was the only way to leave Tuol Sleng: execution at the killing fields. Or death under torture.

The photographer took pictures of those who were tortured to death at the prison too. These photographs are also on display at the museum. Black-and-white, beaten-up bodies. They're lying in rows. Would they want us to be staring at them like this? The people photographed by a man whose name we know, as Susan Sontag points out, "remain an aggregate: anonymous victims."

Do they have to remain anonymous? The executioners, by accident and without thinking—quite unlike first-rate per-petrators of genocide—did a service to the memory of their victims by taking their photographs. They produced records, now preserved on microfilm and inventoried. Thanks to their last-minute portraits, the victims can be remembered individu-ally. If not for the photos, it would be just another mass murder. The pictures give this crime a unique quality. The guides point out individual faces to the tourists, and explain whose eyes are now looking at us. Who this man was, who this woman was. The faces from S-21 have names. Maybe one day the Genocide Museum in Phnom Penh will try to caption each picture. It still seems possible, to some extent. At least this much could be done for the victims. But does it still matter today? Does it have any significance? And for whom?

Nhem Ein, the photographer, gives a detailed account of the Khmer Rouge era as seen from Tuol Sleng prison. Sometimes he left the prison to photograph Pol Pot. Sometimes he merely developed pictures of the leader that were taken by someone else. Once, because of scratches on the film, it looked like Brother Number One had a scar on his face. The photographer almost paid for it with his life. Comrade Duch sent him away to work in the fields. For three months the photographer worked there without knowing if he would live or die, but finally he went back to the prison. And continued to photograph the people who were brought in blindfolded.

His account is solid and well-organized, told day by day, detail by detail, and there's so much information that before our conversation it's hard to find questions that the book doesn't answer. On the final page, the photographer makes an appeal to today's world leaders. An appeal for peace. He mentions Iraq and Syria, Libya and Afghanistan, Israel and Palestine. Lofty words. This is the only part of the book that betrays any emotion.

Nhem Ein should be asked about his emotions. About his tears. About his dreams. About today.

Finally he picks up the phone. "No problem," he says. "I charge five hundred dollars for an interview. It's a reasonable fee."

The Year of All the Deaths

My name is Nhep Sary, I'm a mother, and I don't want anything in exchange for my story.

I live in Phnom Penh. I'll do my best to tell you everything as concisely as I can. I'll leave out lots of details that are too heavy for you to bear. Grief isn't safe. Grief does no one any good. It can deprive you of reason, of the power in your legs, of the breath in your lungs. Grief is dying.

2017. Let's keep things in chronological order, that way it'll be easier for you to get to the end. That's to say, to today, a blazing hot November, when at the age of seventy-three I'm sitting on a chair outside my house not far from the Russian

Market. Here we are, drinking water, eating fruit, and smiling. A lovely moment. You know what, the fruit and vegetables from the market are full of pesticides, especially the imported ones. The local ones are better, but they cost more. So my daughter and I have a small garden here on the roof, a few vegetables, fruits, and herbs. One must eat a healthy diet—please, help yourselves. I might give you some dates, mention the year, one or two of them, though these days I'm not certain of any dates.

1945. I was born long ago in Kandal province, which when viewed from Phnom Penh lies on the opposite bank of the Mekong. My father was a farmer and head of the village for sixteen years. The local people elected him four times, because he always had their best interests at heart. A wise, good, cheerful man. There were eleven of us, four brothers, six sisters, and me—the fifth child. Now I'm the only one left alive.

1950. We were poor, but we had six cows. My parents sold them and bought a wooden house in Phnom Penh. It stood on the water, in the Boeung Keng Kang district, which means "Serpent Living in Water." The house was so small that we couldn't all live in it at once. My parents and the younger children remained in the village, where our father had duties. The five older children went to the city—in other words, I lucked out. My oldest sister was in charge of us, and she cooked our food. She worked at a match factory.

1952. I turned seven, and went to school in the capital. The teacher didn't want to accept me. "You're too little," he said, but I insisted. That was when the French were still here, so by the third year of junior school we all spoke French. That's to say I definitely did, because I was a model student. In the first year I used to draw mango trees, palm trees, and crocodiles. But what do they do nowadays? I can see how limited education has become in my granddaughter's case. She does nothing but coloring. In those days, junior school lasted for six years. Anyone who completed it could become a teacher, a nurse, or a policeman. They were adults by then, of course, because we started junior school at the age of thirteen. I was an exception: I was thirteen when I completed it. Then I went to senior school, a private one. My sister was still working at the match factory. She used to bring glue and cardboard home. In the evenings we made boxes. My record was eighty boxes in four hours.

1960. Our father died. Five years before, he and our mother had moved to the city, into our little house. He used to fetch soil from the Mekong and sell it to people. Momma sold cookies outside the house. The Khmers love sweets. The youngest of my siblings were twin girls. They were around three or four years old, I'm not sure. I remember their little bare butts and Momma's tears. My four other sisters were married off by then. One of our siblings had died earlier of Dengue fever. Momma stayed on at the house with the remaining six of us.

1962. At senior school I was taught history and geography by Mr. Saloth Sar. He used to come to school in a horse-drawn carriage, a closed cab, in which he never opened the vents. He lectured, or rather dictated, in French, straight off the top of his head. He could remember the length of the Danube, the Nile, and the Mississippi. The height of the tallest peaks on every continent. The population of France, Argentina, China. A man made of numbers, a human calculator. I never saw his eyes, because never once did he take off his dark glasses. He wore dark pants, a dark shirt with long sleeves in spite of the heat, never short sleeves like other men. "Open your exercise books,"

he'd say at the start of the lesson, "and write down what I say."
He'd dictate for two hours. He never smiled, he never mentioned
politics—how could he, when he never conversed with us? He
set written tests, then marked and returned them to us without
comment.

1963. We went to the movie house by the river. Several high-
school classes at once. A large auditorium, high-ceilinged, lovely,
well-lit. Suddenly a gendarme blew his whistle, the doors closed,
and the lights went out. I was terrified. It was the first time I had
ever been in a movie house. What was the movie called? I can't
remember the title, or the plot. Just the silence before the movie,
and the darkness.

1964. I passed the exam, spent a year doing teacher training,
and became a teacher. I couldn't get a job in Phnom Penh
because I was unmarried. Only married female teachers could
teach in the capital.

1969. I got married to a teacher. We loved each other. We
asked to be transferred to Phnom Penh. But they gave us posts
in Kandal province. For two years we worked without remu-
neration. We did the job conscientiously. The students had to
write essays at home, compare the protagonists in the assigned
books, and express their own views and ideas. Nowadays, they
apparently don't have to. Nowadays there's no value in having
views of your own. My father-in-law wasn't a Buddhist, but
a Catholic. He knew how to make liquor—I can't remember
what he used, definitely yeast, but it was red and strong. He
drank more alcohol than water, every day, but he had a strong
head, and he never got drunk. When he opened a liquor store
in Phnom Penh, we gave up our jobs at the school, and came
back to help him. Despite the poverty, and the fact that the city

was under siege, the business did well. High-ranking military personnel used to get their supplies from us, General Lon Nol's soldiers, who were defending us against Pol Pot's advancing guerrillas. Help yourselves, it's sweet, fresh pineapple, don't hold back.

1970. I gave birth to my daughter, Srey Oun.

1971. I gave birth to my son, Ane Ang.

1975. On April 17, there was a noise of vehicles from early morning. We opened the door of the store, and saw army trucks with white flags. Then some other trucks without flags. People were cheering and throwing flowers at the feet of the guerrillas. We were pleased. The war was over! "Mother," a boy who knocked on the window addressed me, "Angkar wants you to leave the house. You must all leave. In a short while the Americans are going to bomb the city. Don't take too many things. Angkar says you'll be home again in three days. Angkar is the Supreme Organization. The Organization says this, the Organization says that! Faster! Faster!"

There were a large number of them, armed, and unsmiling. "What should we do?" I asked my husband. "What should we take?" I was afraid for the children, I was in tears. Rice for three days. Clothes for three days. Two pots, a sleeping mat. We threw it all into a car full of bottles of liquor. I hid some jewelry and some cash in my clothing. We set off. I wanted to take my mom, who was still living in the Boeung Keng Kang district, but the insurgents blocked our way. "Go in the opposite direction." There was also an assistant from the store with us. He, my husband, and my father-in-law pushed our car. Had we run out of gas? Or was it because we didn't want to drive too far away from home? I can't remember. "Come on! Come on!"

shouted the guerrillas. "Faster, faster!" And they kept calling me "Mother," and my husband "Father."

On the roadside we saw the first piles of uniforms taken off Lon Nol's soldiers. The first bodies. April, as you know, is the hottest time of year here. That night, traveling in a wide column, we reached the suburbs, in the vicinity of the airport. We started looking for firewood, as I wanted to cook some rice for the children. They were exhausted, almost fainting. I ran into a friend from senior school. Her face was radiant, beaming with enthusiasm. She asked if I was joining our teacher. "What teacher?" "Pol Pot." I already knew that name, of course, but I didn't know he was our Mr. Sar, our former history and geography teacher. "I'll think about it," I told my friend, and went to take care of the children. I wonder if she's still alive today? Or did she end up in Tuol Sleng? Dawn came, the guerrillas told us to keep moving, farther and farther from home. They kept urging us on. We'd run out of rice, but not liquor. For a kilo of rice I traded three bottles, then four. We also had some money, but nobody wanted it. I realized it had no value when I saw banknotes scattered in the road. Then we ran out of liquor. I had some medicine, so I offered it in exchange for rice. Many of the deportees were sick from overheating, malnutrition, hunger, and shock. They were running fevers. But I couldn't help those who had no rice to give me in exchange. I saw lots of bodies by the roadside, in ditches, and the children saw them too—the farther away from Phnom Penh, the more there were. We partly walked and partly drove, altogether for fifteen days and fifteen nights. We reached Takeo. Then the village my mom was from. We went to the Organization to get registered. We lied about our education. My husband said he was a driver. I said I was a housewife. My son was five, and my daughter four. They sent us to work in a rice field.

Three months later we found out my mom ended up at my father's village, where I'd been born. We ran off to her at night, and were there before daybreak. On the way we were stopped by the Organization, which never slept. They asked where we were from. From Phnom Penh. "Why did you take you such a long time to get here?" "Because we were sick along the way." They let us go. We found my mom. They sent us to work in a rice field, but not for long. They knew I was a teacher. And that my younger brother had tried to join Lon Nol's army. They knew everything. And they decided to get rid of us. "Your whole family is going north." Several families: mine, my two sisters' families, and my mom. Twenty-five people in all. Under escort, they took us by train to Pursat. There, carts harnessed to cows were waiting. We drove a short way, then they ordered us to walk. Into the jungle. It was pouring rain. You know what the rains can be like here. That was all we had: trees, and a downpour. No shelter, not a grain of rice. When the rain stopped, we started to build shelters. In silence. And there were some four hundred of us walking around in the jungle. I counted. Then more arrived. A thousand mute people in dense, damp jungle. No one spoke. Everyone was afraid of everyone else. A day, a night, a day, a night. Finally someone brought a sack of rice. Three days later another one. It was too little. We walked for an hour to fetch water from a small lake. We struck fire. We had to have strength. They ordered us to cut down the jungle. We cut it down. There were ever fewer trees around us, and ever more sunlight. My husband made a portable awning for the children out of branches so they'd have a bit of shade. The women caught everything in the lake that was alive. With their bare hands, successfully. They had food for their children. I, a teacher from the city, was incapable of catching anything, everything slipped out of my grasp. I'd be in tears. Someone gave me some crabs, a fish, and I took them, for the children. As I made them soup, I'd be thinking: "These are not our crabs, this is not our fish, we shouldn't be eating them." Then my husband started going to the lake, where he caught a lot, and I had even greater pangs of conscience. Or rather, fear, that they might take my husband away somewhere, and I wouldn't be able to secure food for the children. The Organization lived with us the whole time, and forced us to work. We went out in the morning and came back at night. It wasn't labor, it was torture. They knew we didn't have the strength to last for long. We could tell from the look of the jungle that others had felled it before us. We were afraid we'd end up the same way. A month later, the Organization decided it was taking two hundred people away. "Tomorrow," they said, "you'll be leaving this place. Mothers! Fathers! Get ready for the journey." How were we supposed to get ready? What do you take with you, when you have nothing? Nobody asked any questions. We all kept our mouths shut. Out of terror, which from now on would remain inside us to the end. Even those who survived are still afraid. Every day frightens them. Every stranger. And often their own people too. We wait in terror for the end, just as on that day we waited blankly for the dawn.

Next morning, we were divided into groups of fifty. "Angkar orders you to go east. And you to go west. You people to the north. You to the south." We set off with the entire family, all twenty-five of us still alive. We reached the village of Ta Mok.

1976. The year of all the deaths. I gave birth to a child.

A third one. A son. He died soon after, as did many of the children born to mothers exhausted by labor. Women who were sick and hungry. They say Pol Pot killed close to a million, perhaps two million. Does that include my son who only lived a few hours? The thousands of sons who only lived a few hours, and daughters who only lived a few minutes? Did anyone count those children? These fruits are from our roof garden, please help yourselves. It hasn't rained much lately, though we're in the rainy season. It's not too damp, you don't sweat as much—drink up, you mustn't stint on water. So the village was called Ta Mok. Like Brother Number Five. I don't know where the name came from, perhaps Brother Number Five was born there, or maybe he spent time there. I never saw him, nobody asked about him—who'd have dared? But everyone knew the name was in his honor. I remember talking to my husband about it, though at the time we didn't know that in future years they'd rename him The Butcher. Brother Number Five even imprisoned Pol Pot, shortly before his death. He himself ended up in jail eventually—he died there before the tribunal had had time to pass judgment on him. You probably know about that, I shouldn't gabble so much—help yourselves to fruit. Every morning, the men went to work under the command of a man. The women were managed by a woman. Eight hours in the rice fields. That's to say nine, because we had our food with us. Each person brought their own small pot. And when the sun was at its zenith, the commanders announced a break. No shade.

Now about the meal. I have a lot to say on the topic, because thanks to my pregnancy they allowed me not to go to the field. I was put in charge of the kitchen. I had 450 people to feed. That's how many of us there were in Ta Mok, at the beginning.

Every day the commandant told me how many little cups of rice I could tip into thirteen gallons of water. Five or ten cups for all those people. I poured a mug of cloudy water for each person into a small pot. Each person had to receive a portion of rice. If anyone went without, I'd be punished. I'd quietly do the calculations: the pot held thirteen gallons, and a mug for each hungry mouth held almost a pint . . . I couldn't show that I knew how to count. The Organization was watching my hands the whole time. The Organization, that's to say some boys: they were thirteen years old, with cold, stern eyes that followed my every move. To see if I was pouring equally, or giving more to my own family. Those who hadn't found a snail or a worm to eat, and relied only on the rice, were among the first to die. We were all sick. We had no medicine. Every day my husband walked six miles to work. He was building a dam on the river. Pol Pot did a lot of construction work there, he was creating new lakes. I stayed with the children. I was in the kitchen, and they were at pre-school, in the care of the old people. Any child who reached the age of seven had to go to work. The rice had heavy ears, and it looked as if there'd be plenty of it, but there wasn't. Nobody summoned me when my daughter was dying. When my son was dying, I was standing over him. I ran to the village head to help me. "Commander! My son is dying!" "Wait," he said. "We'll wait until several of them have died, then carry them up together." He was talking about a nearby hill. That was where they carried the bodies, toward the end of the day, and buried them in shallow pits. At night, wolves came and dug up those graves. The wolves ate my children's bodies.

My children died before they had to work. Today they'd be approaching fifty. In just a few months, from 450 we were reduced to 350. My older sister, whose name was Nhep Sithan, her husband and their five children all died, one by one. I can't remember exactly when. And my younger twin sisters. They were eighteen years old. First the one who was studying science at university. Then the one who was training to be a teacher, and who kept a journal in English. She wrote a daily account of what the Organization was doing to us. From leaving Phnom Penh to the very end. She'd brought some exercise books and pencils from home. I didn't know where she hid them. I wasn't with her when she died. She told a friend the exercise books were on the roof, and the friend told me. I immediately ran to look for them, but they were all wet, the letters couldn't be saved. If only she'd kept them under her pillow . . . If I had those exercise books today, I'd give them to you for publication. But they were lost. Let at least her name survive: Nhep Sarin. Her twin was Nhep Sareth. My mom was Phan Souk. Because Mom died too, straight after. And my husband, Prak Buthan. He held out, he passed on responsibly, last of all, after the children. He injured his foot on the dam construction site, developed an infection, weakened, his leg swelled up, went septic, and I lost him. Of twenty-five relatives, there were five of us left. Me, one sister, and her three children. What would you have done in my place?

1977. Who cares about the fortunes of an old teacher from Cambodia? I should tell you my story without so many details— please keep an eye on me, to make sure I speak succinctly. There was a rapid river there, the one on which my husband had been building the dam. And I was still young. Whenever I wanted to jump, I'd hear my mom's voice: there's damnation in store for anyone who takes their own life. I didn't jump. But I still wanted to. One day, I woke up hungry. There were trees laden with oranges growing all around us. We all knew the Organization guarded them non-stop. Off I went. Let them shoot me. "Thief!" shouted this guy, though I hadn't touched a single fruit. He put a pistol to my head. He had his finger on the trigger as he ordered me to go away. I was sure he'd shoot me in the back. I didn't dare look behind me. He didn't shoot. All right, Mom, I thought, I'll go on living.

I'm telling you half the story. If I told you everything, my heart would break. Of three hundred fifty, there were one hundred of us left in Ta Mok. The commander decided I should be moved. "You're off to another village," he said, "because everyone's going to die here." I didn't want to leave my sister and her children. "You're going where there's more food," insisted the commander. I couldn't believe he was concerned about me. When they took people off into the unknown, it certainly wasn't to save their lives. We all knew that. But I accepted his decision. I was reconciled with the end. If that's it, then all right, I thought, let them kill me there. I'll be following my children and my husband. I got on a cart harnessed to cows. It wasn't far. The village was called Peanic. There was a warehouse for rice, dried fish, and salt. The new commander asked if it was true that I was a teacher. Of course not! But I saw someone I knew hovering nearby. My student. She belonged to the Organization. I was an instructor, I said, because an instructor was inferior, a sort of not-fully-qualified teacher. He didn't believe me. And gave me a job as a team leader. I couldn't refuse. Any sort of objection meant death. Now I was in charge of some other women. They did sewing. Every day, each of the six seamstresses had to hand in at least two black uniforms. If she made fewer than that, she was punished. And so was I. Other teams wove baskets for carrying earth, or made bowls out of metal, by hand. One team produced buckets. That was where Kon Nan worked.

He said that before Pol Pot he'd been a construction worker. A schoolteacher, the Organization decided, and a worker will make a good combination. A good couple. "You're going to be husband and wife." We met at supper. I don't know what he was like, what impression he made on me. I remember what he said: "Don't argue, don't protest." I hadn't a thought in my head. Except for one: anyone who refuses to agree to a marriage arranged by the Organization dies. Excuse me, I'm going into the kitchen for a while, I'll make some tea—I've got to think about something else.

I'm sorry I was gone so long. I've brought some cookies— here, please help yourselves. A week later, one evening they summoned me, and they summoned him. "Sit down," said the commander. We sat down without a word. "Stand up, hold hands." We stood up and held hands. "Repeat after me: I take this woman to be my wife." Kon Nan repeated it. "I take this man to be my husband." I repeated it. "That's all," said the commander. But it wasn't all, because they immediately announced that we had to get going. Why on earth the wedding, if death were coming that same night? The Organization took various strange decisions. Why try to figure out their logic?

"You're going back to Ta Mok!"

The place where my children died? It hadn't even been a year. The place where my husband died?

We didn't argue. We each took a cooking pot, and walked into the darkness, into the rain. My new husband walked ahead—he didn't wait for me, or pay me any attention. At one point I fell off a footbridge into a canal, I was bruised, and soaked to the skin. He didn't stop for an instant. We reached Ta Mok before dawn. The roosters were crowing. "I couldn't help you," he said, "because the Organization was walking with us. Concern for my new wife? Why on earth show them that sort of emotion?"

We were sent to work in the fields.

1978. You probably feel awkward about asking—we slept together like brother and sister. In a hut on pillars. The Organization slept under the floor. Were they listening to hear if we were sleeping together like husband and wife? I doubt it. They checked we weren't quarrelling. We didn't talk at all, so we had no arguments either. Just silence. Every night, silence. Finally, the spies were sure there was nothing suspicious going on between us, and went off to spy on others. During the day we pretended to be a normal couple. That's to say we never showed each other bad feelings. Good ones even less. He wasn't happy either, they'd forced him into it too. Someone who knew me asked if I loved him. "Naturally!" I replied.

Fear of death never left us for an instant.

Until one night we heard footsteps. Thousands of footsteps outside our straw hut. Hundreds of people in black uniforms. Walking in silence. And they went by the next night too. Men or women? Mute, black shadows, once again before dawn, and before the next one, once again in the same direction. To the north-west. Who were the people in black? Why were so many of them on the march? Where to? What for? Definitely for nothing good. We heard rifles, bombs, and an order: "You must go too! The Vietnamese are coming from the south-east. They'll cut your throats."

We set off toward the Cardamom Mountains.

There we felt we could talk. "I don't love you," I said to him. "I don't love you," he said to me. I told him about my children and my husband. He told me about his wife and child. We didn't talk about our brothers and sisters. We understood each other.

1979. He'd been a captain in Lon Nol's army. Now that Pol Pot had fled into the jungle, he could tell me the truth. He wasn't a worker, but a mechanical engineer. I'd suspected at first sight that he was educated. I didn't like soldiers. They carried weapons and were usually stand-offish. Was he? He had a difficult character, unsentimental. I'm emotional. And proud. "We've done a good job," I said "We've survived. Now you can divorce me." He didn't respond at all. A reserved man.

In May we arrived in Phnom Penh. Although four months had gone by since the fall of Pol Pot, there was hardly anyone in the city. We found a small apartment, not far from here. It was empty, so we went in. I got a job at a school. My husband got one at the ministry of agriculture. Had we decided to remain a married couple? We never had that conversation.

1980. I counted the people I had known before Pol Pot. For every ten, two had survived. For example, I used to know a popular actress. These days I know her son. His father and sister were actors too. They were all recognized by the Organization, and they were all killed. Now the actress's son gives people rides on a motorbike for a dollar a time. Earlier, such downward mobility was quite unthinkable. Everything changed after Pol Pot. Especially people. Once upon a time, they helped each other. Nowadays, if they see a thief in the neighbors' garden, they avert their gaze because it's not their problem.

1981. I gave birth to a daughter. She lives in the United States. By the time she was born, her father and I had realized that life together was easier. But neither he, nor I would have wished a compulsory marriage on anyone. You can't force a person to have desires, to feel passion. In front of others, and even in front of ourselves we pretended to be a happy couple.

1985. I gave birth to a second daughter. Now she works in Phnom Penh for a global television company. Does she ever ask about my other children? About their father? No. I think she doesn't want to cause me pain. I do tell my daughters about the year of all the deaths. But never from start to finish. It's always just a small piece, a little bit, very briefly.

1988. My husband had a motorbike accident. Smashed the back of his skull. The hospitals couldn't save people, the doctors didn't know how to do any complicated operations. So he died. Since then, I've been receiving treatment for my heart, for high blood pressure. The second misfortune in my life. Another loss. I couldn't accept it. Why had this happened, when it wasn't I who chose the man? Why on earth, when it was Mr. Sar who'd arranged for me to live with him? In the past, the parents decided who their children would marry. No one dared argue. Not like now, when you're free to choose your own husband. At that time there were no parents. There was the Organization. There was Pol Pot. My younger daughter can't remember her father, and the older one only has a vague memory of him. Very occasionally they ask about him. I tell them he was an honest man, hard-working.

1998. Mr. Saloth Sar died. My teacher, who killed three of my children, my husband, my mom, my older sister and her family, my younger twin sisters, and my brothers. Didn't I tell you about my brothers? Mr. Sar survived all of them by twenty-two years. And my compulsory husband by ten. I'd like to understand why Mr. Sar did so much killing. And why his own people. I'd like to get to the bottom of his heart.

2017. Today, every house in Phnom Penh is surrounded by stone walls, covered with broken glass set into concrete. There are bars sticking out of the gates like pitchforks. There are entanglements between neighbors. Barbed wire stretched along the balconies, on the terraces, on the roofs, even on the trees you could climb to get into a property, or into an upstairs window. People are afraid of people.

You say the people here don't touch each other? That's an interesting observation. And correct. The social customs in Cambodia were always full of taboos, shame, and embarrassment. Before Pol Pot as well. We don't greet each other the way they do in the TV shows, we don't kiss each other on the cheek, we don't embrace. Good day, and that's it. We're even cool toward friends or relatives whom we haven't seen for a long time. Since Pol Pot, we're even cooler. Pol Pot blocked people's emotions, he shut them up inside us, like a cork stopping up a bottle. After Pol Pot we didn't even hug our own new children. Our new children are cold.

Tears? I lost my tears before my first children died. I didn't cry when their bodies were carried up the hill. I didn't cry for my husband. I didn't cry for my mom. I knew I should, but I had no tears. I couldn't find them. To this day I don't know where my tears have gone. When did I lose them? Was it in the village of Ta Mok, or earlier on, in the damp jungle? You say the Khmers don't cry nowadays either? That's an accurate observation. Weeping is an expression of weakness, and people here can't allow themselves to appear weak. To have a moment of help-lessness. They're poor, they work from dawn to dusk, they keep busy in order to survive. The poor man who weeps will perish. Weeping is a luxury. For a pauper, it's suicide. That's if you mean the younger ones. Because for the older people it would be a sort of solution: to drown in your own tears. But for years the eyes of the old Khmers have been as dry as a bone. Dried up once and for all. We're incapable of weeping. And at this point I think I'll say: forgive me. That's enough memories. Grief is dangerous. Let's end my chatter on that note. Do you know by now, how I cope with the past? How does a person manage to live after death without going insane?

Our Culture

"Rape?" wonder the psychologists who work at the Transcultural Psychosocial Organization. That's their response to the question of whether or not forced marriage meant rape.

"No one in Cambodia sees it that way. No one thinks like that. In the past, though not so long ago, parents decided who their daughter would marry, and chose wives for their sons. That was the rule. There were occasional exceptions. And suicides among the newlyweds. Though rarely. Today almost everyone in Cambodia is the child of mothers and fathers who didn't know each other before the wedding. A wife did not expect love from her husband, nor did he expect it from her. That's how it is in our culture. Marriage was a form of commerce, a transaction, a contract. It probably still happens that way in many parts of the country today. More in the countryside than in the towns. They're not forced, but arranged marriages. That's what we call them.

We live in a culture where there's a lack of choice. A daughter is told by her parents: you belong to this man, you must agree, don't argue. So the women didn't protest when Pol Pot forced them to marry. Because the Organization was their mother and father. They wanted to stay alive. So the marriages went ahead. Thousands of forced marriages. Because we do call the ones from Pol Pot's time forced marriages. It was also hard to dissolve those marriages afterward, because divorce isn't part of our tradition. A divorced woman is done for. Sometimes people pity divorcees, but usually they discriminate against them, reject and blame them: you're a bad mother, you were no good at taking care of your family. So the forced wives stayed in those marriages. Some are stuck in them to this day. If the husbands are alive, because many, if not most, have died off by now. Destroyed by the war, or by alcohol and lack of hope. The women who were forced to marry never speak of rape. Even during therapy. Rape is a stigma, like everywhere else in the world. Who'd want to live with a stigma?"

And the children?

"Who'd want to be a child born of rape? Those children are over thirty years old now. The forced wives of the Pol Pot era often failed to give birth. None of them wanted to engender life. And the men didn't have the strength for sex in those days. They were impotent. Children from forced marriages were only born later on. Usually several in each family. Today their old parents don't explain to them what they were forced to do. And as adults the children don't ask about it. Nor do the grandchildren."

Who forced them into marriage? Where are the executioners?

"The genocide in Cambodia wasn't committed by neighbors. The killers didn't come from next door, from across the fence.

They came from a different province. Strangers, unfamiliar people. When the killing ended, everyone went home. Today the Khmer don't know who their neighbors were then, murderers or victims. What did he do in Pol Pot's time? He says, if he says anything at all, that he suffered, he starved, he nearly died. Everyone here nearly died. So who tortured us? Who took life? No one knows. And if something is known, if something comes to light, it's always the same old story: I was just carrying out orders, I just blindfolded people, I just took their photos shortly before the end. I was a victim! There are no executioners in Cambodia, although they're all around us. The executioners live among the survivors. Or inside the survivors. There's both executioner and victim in one and the same body. They see each other every day. On the street, at the market, at work, in the mirror."

What about karma?

"We Khmers regard ourselves as Buddhists, we hold rituals and ceremonies. But we don't understand their meaning. We don't know the teachings of Buddha. Of course we've heard that you mustn't kill or harm any living creature. We've heard that you mustn't steal. Or live a dissolute life. Or tell lies. Or use mind-altering substances. Yes, people believe that if you do good to another person, the good will come back to you, it might even bring you a profit. But if you do harm to another person, you're sure to be paid back in kind. People here don't care about karma. Our Buddhism is sham, just folklore, fakery, and hypocrisy. Buddhism hasn't protected us against anything. We've harmed each other, because we're human beings."

How does the violence of the past affect ordinary life today?

"The Khmer Rouge finally fled into the jungle and fought against Hun Sen's soldiers. Both sides were fighting for the country. When the fighting ended, they were left with nothing. Meaning they were left with depression, which often goes hand in hand with alcohol. Alcoholism is the national problem that Cambodia can't see. Death on the roads, aggression, neighbors breaking each other's skulls with rocks. Each new generation inherits that trauma. Each new generation experiences violence, a lack of affection, a lack of trust, or of a safe touch. We are a society of lonely, abandoned people. We have abandoned each other. It's not long since we all took part in unimaginable, irreversible violence. It was allowed to happen, it was okay. In those days nobody ever asked anyone else: 'How are you, how are you feeling?' And no one ever told anyone else about their feelings. Because everyone was the enemy. And there was no one from abroad here. Khmers murdered Khmers. Though not just Khmers, because we have minorities here. They suffered too. To this day people are still asking: why? How was it possible? Brother informed on, tortured, and killed brother. But no one stops to think about these important questions. Those who were children at the time still live in the belief that aggression is a way of communicating with others. By shouting. Those children weren't given the peace and quiet that children should have. The safety. Their psychological and physical needs weren't met. Today those children are adults. They're like machines transmitting violence. Today, only one in nine children in Cambodia doesn't experience physical violence. So says the research. Children are hit, pushed, yanked, and kicked. They probably all witness violence. Violence at home, violence next door, violence on the way to school, on television, on the internet. We post pictures on Facebook showing car crashes and accidents on construction sites. Bloodstained bodies, alive and dead. Victims of drowning—people often drown here. Murder victims. Summary justice. People often mete out instant justice on their own behalf here because they don't trust the police or the courts. They settle scores, or take revenge. Since Pol Pot, we're good at that, though over half of us were born after his time. We've inherited an obsession with violence. We can't live without violence. The details are visible on the screen: a severed leg, a smashed head, the brains showing. People don't know the meaning of ethics. How could they? What about the victim's right to privacy? I found him, his bloodstained body is mine. His corpse is ours. It's the same in the daily papers, violence is an attraction, there's a stream of fresh blood on morning TV every day."

"The children of Pol Pot's time pass on mistrust to the children of today. 'Mind who you hang out with.' 'Don't shoot your mouth off.' 'Don't express your personal views.' 'Don't stick your neck out.' 'Don't ask questions—what's the point of knowing too much?' 'Don't have close friends.' 'Don't wear such short skirts. You'll only have yourself to blame when something happens to you.' 'Come back before nightfall.' 'Stay at home. You're only safe at home.' 'You're only safe with the family. Everything, and everyone, outside the home is hostile.' 'We're helpless. We have no influence on life, but we must survive it. That means having something to eat and knowing how to hide food.'"

"But it's not always like that. Sometimes it's not survival that matters most, but freedom, fun. 'We had nothing when we were growing up,' say our parents, 'but forced labor and fear. So get the best out of life, child! Don't lose what we lost. Take advantage of your youth.' Parents don't talk to their children about their feelings—as we all know, they can't do it. But they're happy to buy the child a scooter. As long as they can afford it. Money is a way of expressing parental love. 'Eat, have fun!' It often ends badly. Drugs, rape, the everyday reality that we don't talk about."

"But when something does go wrong, it's not their daughter who's to blame, or their son. It's an outsider. Everyone in Cambodia has their own handy outsider. 'It was the woman next door who told her to go there.' 'It was the neighbor who had a bad influence on him.' People have to have an enemy. We don't know how to breathe without an enemy. We're never to blame for anything, we're never responsible. It's always him or her that's to blame, the enemy. 'It wasn't the Khmers who wanted to kill the Khmers, the Chinese forced us to do it. America bombarded us before that. And before that the French oppressed the Khmers for decades. No one wished us well. Finally, the Vietnamese rescued us, they drove Pol Pot out of Phnom Penh, but not to help us, just to take control of Cambodia. To rule over us. The new authorities are happy to manipulate us too. Who is responsible for our poverty and our sicknesses? The Vietnamese! We all hate the Vietnamese here. Yesterday I consumed chemicals that did me harm. That's to say: I ate vegetables imported from Vietnam. They sprinkle chemicals on them specially to poison us all.'"

What about the art of conversation?

"Every conversation is stressful. People don't listen to each other. They can't hear what's going on around them. And they use words that are as sharp as knives. Teachers shout at their pupils. Bosses shout at their staff. At the market, you pick up a cauliflower and ask how much it costs. You hear a price that sounds too high. So you put it back. To which the vendor says that if you don't want it, you can fuck off. If it's a woman who picks up the cauliflower and puts it back, by way of farewell she'll be told she's a stupid whore."

What about women in Cambodia?

"They often get told they're stupid. 'The fuck you know! You're an idiot'—that's the model for communication between husband and wife. The husband hits the wife: 'Because you don't obey me! You drive me up the wall!' The research shows that one in three women is abused by her partner. But as we're well aware, it's more like one in three is not abused. Or one in four. The more children she has, the more a woman gets hit. She's more dependent on the man. Domestic violence doesn't shock anyone here because it's an expression of love. Very few beaten wives seek help from their parents, but they often don't find it there. 'He's your husband,' they're told, 'you have to live with him, not with us.' Marriage changes domestic violence into something natural, permissible. That's usually what the beaten wife thinks, too. Then she sees a social campaign on huge billboards, saying it's a crime. She understands: 'I'm a victim.' But she won't report her husband. What if he ends up in prison? The family and neighbors will never forgive her for informing on him. Nor will her own children. Children without a father are stigmatized and outcast. Children without a father are inferior, humiliated. We're extremely good at humiliating each other here. But we don't know how to support or love each other."

Do Cambodians declare love to each other?

"Maybe somewhere it does happen occasionally. But it's not the norm. Children aren't told by their parents that they're loved. So they don't say: 'I love you, Mom.' Or: 'I love you, Dad.' How are they to know you can express your feelings like that? Here everyone thinks a child whose mother or father tells it that it's loved is bound to be spoiled: 'My mom loves me, so I don't have to do anything.' If no one has ever told you as a child that they love you, how are you going to say it to your future wife, husband, or children?"

What about hugging?

"This is not the West—in our country there's no touching. A correct observation. Our boss, Dr. Sotheara, goes abroad, then comes back and tells us we should hug our children. That hugging within the family is a good way to communicate, an expression of intimacy, love, and security. So we try to hug our children, but not when anyone else is looking. In Cambodia, hugging, stroking, caressing, holding hands, or any sort of touching that isn't hitting, looks like a sexual gesture. At the very least it's embarrassing, too personal. That's why when married couples greet each other at the airport in Phnom Penh after a long separation they never touch. There's no kiss, no embrace, or show of affection. Kissing at the airport only happens in American films. The importance of hugging is probably described in European magazines, but nobody reads them here."

What about reading?

"Forty years ago reading carried a risk of death. 'Why on earth are you reading?' say today's parents who were children then. Many of them can't spell a single word because they never went to school. And now they warn their own children: 'You'll fall under the influence of what you find out from books, or from the newspaper. Watch out! Better do something more important, something useful.' The level of critical thinking is universally low here. Intellectual capital is weak. We graduated in psychology, we treat people, but we don't read books. We don't talk about books. Are there books in Khmer, you ask? There are books about good nutrition, but I don't think there's any literature, philosophy, history, or politics. The internet? The only thing online in Khmer that's genuine is the violence on Facebook. People search for violence on the internet. And pornography. They don't discuss serious things on Facebook. What would they talk about? We don't discuss politics, we don't argue about it. How can we have a debate when we're afraid to let our own neighbors know who we voted for? We're afraid to breathe in front of our neighbors."

That about sums up our conversations with the psychologists and therapists at the TPO. Their names are: Sok Phaneth, Om Chariya, Hoy Vathan, and Seang Leap, with whom we've been visiting the confined patients.

Baksbat

"Get over it?" says Dr. Sotheara Chhim—psychiatrist and director of the TPO and boss to Dr. Ang Sody and the above-mentioned psychologists—as he invites us into his office. "It's not that simple in Cambodia. 'All that' is still smoldering behind our smiles. The Khmer smile is a facade. We're consumed by grief. People don't have the strength to worry about the past because they have to worry about today. There are children, they have to be fed. But you only have to stop for a moment amid the daily rush, and take a closer look, to see that all that is still present, it hasn't gone away. That's why we're still suffering here. For a long time we didn't talk to each other about it. Nobody told us we must. We were afraid to talk. Today too, people are afraid of people, they're always on the alert, tense, aching. Everyone's a victim. Or an executioner. No one knows who is which. The tribunal got under way to judge the criminals. How can I help my mother when I see her crying? She watches the television, and she sees Comrade Duch, the commander of Tuol Sleng prison, testifying in court with his head raised. The younger people pay no attention to the executioner's words—they don't have the time. Or the curiosity. They're not capable of talking to their elders about all that. The young people can't feel it. They don't believe the older generation could have experienced anything as cruel. How did they survive, if it was impossible to survive? There was too much of it for anyone to believe it or comprehend it today. Let my mother do her crying, and not watch the tribunal anymore. It's a pity, because in Cambodia we don't live long. Anyone who can remember the Khmer Rouge is like a rich archive of historical information today. Altogether, there are thousands of these archives, but they're all going to collapse soon. The elderly are passing on. Their unrecorded life stories will be lost. We're losing ourselves. The young people don't think all that affects them. But they're wrong. We're all being brought down by passivity, apathy, *baksbat*."

Baksbat—broken courage syndrome.

According to Dr. Sotheara, it's a disorder that's only apparent in Cambodia. It's a cultural syndrome involving compound trauma, a dangerous disorder that's hereditary and universal here. He has written several academic works about it. We talk at length on the topic, a number of times, in his office. Everything he has written and told us can be summarized as follows:

◆   The Venerable Chuon Nath, deceased Buddhist
    Supreme Patriarch of Cambodia and author of the

first dictionary of the Khmer language, explained that *baksbat* is derived from the noun *bak*, meaning "breaking off," or "fracture." And from the noun *sbat*, meaning "body," or "form." In Khmer, people often use compound nouns or alliteration to reinforce the meaning of words. So the word *sbat* can also be used in the term *sbat-sbov*. In this case, sbat is an adjective, meaning "thick," or "dense." And the noun *sbov* means "thatch," or a kind of grass that the Khmer peasants use as a roof covering. The patriarch Chuon Nath said that whenever an elephant touches dense thatch (or walks across thick grass), the original form of the thatch or grass is destroyed forever. *Baksbat* is the permanent destruction of the body or soul. In the first dictionary it is defined as "broken courage."

⁎ The term *baksbat* has probably been present in the Khmer language since the fall of Angkor and the Khmer Empire in 1431, following the invasion of the Siamese from the West. That defeat prompted *baksbat* in the local people.

⁎ It's a pain that cannot be cured, so it's passed on through the generations.

⁎ Some Cambodian historians describe the Khmers as "an ethnic group with *baksbat*," because there's been suffering here for centuries as a result of wars with the neighbors, and cruel living conditions under repressive regimes, in the colonial era as well as later on. Today, many of those questioned within research into broken courage syndrome believe that *baksbat* was passed on to them from the previous generation.

- *Baksbat* is a sense of fear that hasn't left following a trauma.

- Trauma may include the death of a loved one, watching the pain of a loved one, shell shock, captivity, labor beyond one's capacities, starvation, torture, rape, a land mine accident, encountering a ghost, or being chased by a wild animal.

- Another definition of *baksbat* is "feeling afraid for centuries."

- Or: "damaged spine."

- A person with *baksbat* feels as if they'll never regain their former peace.

- They feel as if they'll never laugh again.

- They have no initiative. They can't make decisions.

- They give in easily. After an initial defeat, they won't take up a challenge again.

- They'd rather die than make another attempt.

- They don't know how to defend themselves.

- They can't rely on themselves.

- They won't tell others about their defeats.

- Some Cambodian psychiatrists and psychologists equate *baksbat* with post-traumatic stress disorder (PTSD), because both disorders feature the same symptoms. The patient is constantly reliving their old trauma. It's with them in their dreams, and when they're awake. It's not a memory, it's the present time. The trauma goes on, but the patient refuses to talk about it. They feel abandoned, they withdraw from contact with people, take a negative view of the future, sleep badly, have frequent bursts of rage, have trouble concentrating, and are extremely oversensitive. And yet the specialists perceive differences between the Western PTSD and the Khmer broken courage syndrome. The symptoms of *baksbat* that aren't present in PTSD, or aren't as intense, include surrendering easily, mistrust, servility, and submissiveness.

- If asked their name, a person with *baksbat* is afraid to introduce themselves. To survive Pol Pot, these people had to change their names. To this day, they've never gone back to their real ones.

- A person with *baksbat* doesn't want to be conspicuous.

- They don't help other people because they're afraid of them.

- Kong Bunchoeun, a famous writer here, drew up a list of more than forty kinds of illness among the Khmers. He thinks *baksbat* is one; to this day, those who saw people killed by the American air raids are suffering from it, as are those who saw Pol Pot's guerrillas tying people up and murdering them.

- When people with *baksbat* encounter someone who is their superior, they immediately bow their heads, their hearts beat faster, and their bodies tremble with fear. They don't dare to speak, and they're afraid of accusations and retaliation. They prefer to keep silent. If they must say something, they praise those who rank above them, they crawl and suck up to them. When a powerful person farts, his inferiors say they can smell perfume. Those suffering from *baksbat* are afraid that if an important person dislikes them, or something about them, for any reason, they'll perish.

+ Cultural norms demand obedience to one's elders. That was always in evidence here. Under the Khmer Rouge, it changed into submissiveness. No one had the right to refuse to carry out a guard's orders. The guard could torture and kill whenever he felt like it.

+ People with *baksbat* easily let themselves be dominated.

+ They'd rather die than stand up for themselves.

+ According to traditional healers, *baksbat* can mean the loss of a soul. Souls jump out of the body, or move to the tips of the person's hair. Because in Cambodia people believe we have nineteen small souls and one big one. When the small souls are lost without trace, a person loses consciousness. A psychiatrist might compare their state with a state of dissociation, depersonalization, or derealization. But according to the healers it's even worse when the big soul is lost. Then the person goes insane. And spends years dying.

• *Baksbat* can affect an entire society. The residents of a building or a village who experience the same trauma (being evicted from their homes, for instance, or mass infection with an illness) don't get organized, they don't protest, or defend their rights.

+ Along with patronage (let us remember the brick-works), *baksbat* has created people in Cambodia who cannot imagine a future. Why would they, when they're convinced they have no influence over it? Their rights don't belong to them, so they can't defend them. That's why they so often let themselves be exploited by others, and by the authorities.

- *Baksbat* prevents the sufferer from taking a step forward—it only allows them to go backward.

- If for years on end people haven't the courage to support what's fair, and to stand up against what's not, successive generations grow up blind to human injustice, and deaf to the suffering of others. Vast numbers of insensitive people.

- A society in which, apart from the family, there are no ties.

- A society, but not a community.

- *Baksbat* is the killer of communities.

- People don't trust the regime, but they don't want to change it. The one that's in power isn't doing any killing. And change means risk: they might tie us up or blindfold us again.

There's one thing Dr. Sotheara doesn't talk about: this regime does occasionally lock people up, and sometimes it shoots at them. For example, at the seamstresses who went on strike in January 2014.

OPERATION UNCHAIN

Talan.

She gazes at the treetops, communes with the birds, and has a teenage son born of rape. Every day the boy hears his mother behaving like a bird in a cage, warbling, trilling, and twittering. Does she love her son? Is she aware of his existence?

The cage, built with the money donated by Khmers from America, is the pride of her father, who started healing people after his encounter with an angel. Today, when we arrive, Talan is still sitting locked inside it. But some time has passed since our last visit. The grass around the cage has grown, the bushes are thicker, nature is waiting for the rain. The patient has put on weight, she's calmer, and apparently she's been saying individual words: water, drink, eat, hot, cold, dark. It's not much after a year's treatment—Dr. Sody is disappointed. Where's the father? He hasn't even come to talk to the doctor. He just acts the saint—Leap, the psychologist, is unhappy about it too. "He says he helps people, as a kru khmer, but he hasn't any time for his own sick daughter. That's not the Buddhist way." And there's conflict with his sister, Talan's aunt. She's the one who takes care of the young woman. She feeds and washes her and gives her the medicine. Regularly? We don't know, because strange things keep happening to the medicine. It's been almost a year since the night when someone threw all the pills into Talan's cage at once. Sixty of them. Luckily, she didn't take a single one. When the aunt arrived in the morning with a bowl of rice, she noticed the pills scattered about, and picked them all up. But she can't explain how they got there. Had someone taken them from her house? Was someone trying to get rid of Talan?

Is she safe when night falls and deprives her prison of light? The darkness falls very quickly here, but the noises don't stop as suddenly. The dogs howl, the monkeys laugh, the owls hoot, the frogs croak, the insects buzz, and the wind rattles, whistles, and shudders.

Everyone sits at home, for fear of night spirits, apparitions, and phantoms. Most of all the flying head known as the arp. This monster takes human form—it appears as a woman with a charming face, but with deep-set red eyes, because she sleeps when the sun is shining, but she's so beautiful that no man can walk past her indifferently. At night her head separates from her body, red and blue veins and arteries hang down from her neck like the arms of an octopus, she feeds on pigswill and dead dogs, she flies fast, and with her long tongue spreads disease among people in their sleep. She glows bright red, thanks to which the farmers who get up before dawn can see her in the rice fields, devouring fat toads for her breakfast. She's hungry. For at night she failed to track down a new-born human baby—that's her favorite meal.

In Cambodia, the arp is a very well-known monster. They say many a man has woken at daybreak and been horrified to see that his wife has no head. But when the sun comes up, the beautiful head goes back to its place. These are the sort of stories people tell here. Everyone's afraid of nocturnal monsters—no one sets foot out of doors at night.

Can't anyone hear Talan's cries at night? Is there nobody here after dark? Surely anyone can creep through the dense, black bushes without being heard?

"Yes, they can," says Leap the psychologist. "The patient is easy prey for evildoers."

A month ago, the packet of pills disappeared from the house yet again. The aunt ran to the cage but couldn't find it. Had Talan swallowed them? There was no sign of that; she was just the same as usual. This time someone had stolen the pills to stop her from taking them. The aunt called the TPO for help. Dr. Sody sent new medicine by courier. What did Talan's father say? "He wasn't bothered. He's a bad man," says his sister. "He's quite capable of hitting me. And he'll lay into his daughter when she shouts or bangs against the bars."

What's going on between father and daughter? "Our minds are not at rest about it," says Leap, scratching his head. "But we don't know anything for certain. Is the aunt telling us the truth? The whole truth? Is she hiding something? She refuses to complain to the police."

We're standing around the cage, where Talan is squatting. She doesn't notice us.

Mr. Tuol Sleng has been freed!

The shackle has been removed from his leg. And not that long ago, his wife thought he'd be better off dead. "I'll never release him," she'd said. The patient was given the first pills from Dr. Sody four months ago.

"What's your name?" the doctor asks him.

"My name is Hap," he replies with a full sentence.

"Do you sleep at night?"

"Yes."

"No one bothers you?"

"No."

"No one comes after you?"

"No."

"What about food?"

"I eat. I'm always hungry."

"When are you given rice?"

"When the sun is high, and in the evening."

"Do you wash?"

"Yes, every few days."

"Do they give you medicine?"

"Yes."

Some time after the start of the treatment, the husband said to his wife: "Release me."

She was astonished. He had never uttered a request of this kind before, or at least no one in the family could remember him doing so. How could he, when not long after his imprisonment he had gone completely mute. All those years without a word, shut away in a world to which no one had access. Until suddenly, quietly but distinctly, two words at once.

Release me.

Does the recovering patient understand his wretched situation?

Though released, he won't go far. After twenty years of sitting on a board, he can't stand up. His withered legs won't obey him anymore. So his wife and son decided it was time to restore his freedom. Because they were afraid he'd die, still chained to that rod, but never leave. He'd become a kmouch—a hungry ghost. Angry, vengeful, unaware that its body is dead. But it'll cast off the shackle, get up from the board, stalk around the house, and haunt the family. So Mr. Hap's son tells us today. Mr. Hap's wife says nothing, as if now she's the one who has gone mute. In the end they took off the shackle.

But it wasn't easy, because it had rusted. The neighbors came running to help with a hammer. Others came running to watch. They're not afraid of Hap's former anger; even if it did come back one day, he could no longer burn down anyone's house. They can see that although he's been set free, he's still in prison. His movements are restricted by an invisible rod. A couple of feet to the left and back again.

"Are you free?" asks Dr. Sody.

"Yes."

"Are you pleased?"

"Yes. But my leg hurts."

"Where does it hurt?"

"Under the shackle."

The sun blazes. Mr. Hap sits, just as he sat the last time we saw him, under a straw awning. Beside him there's a haystack, a cow, and an even row of rustling palm trees the height of a tower block. But the awning has been improved, it's wider. Instead of a narrow board, there's a narrow kre. The son has made an effort. But the wife hasn't, really. That's the doctor's assessment of her today. "You don't take care of your husband," she tells the white-haired woman in a steely tone. "You don't give him enough to eat."

The psychologist adds a few warm remarks. He talks about respect, dignity, and the law. The white-haired woman manages to utter three or four words, and promises change: she'll feed her husband better. The doctor forewarns that she'll be visiting them again in a while. And tells us on the side: "Maybe she'll take him into the house, maybe Hap will return to the family."

That would be good. That is the goal the doctor and the psychologist set themselves in each case: to return the patient to life within the family. Going back into the house heals. Will the wife find room for her disabled husband in her windowless straw cottage? Once they were in love with each other, then, though close, they lived further and further apart: torturer and victim. Who was who? Who inflicted the pain? Who suffered? Will the released husband be given just a little space in his wife's life? Is it really fair to expect that of her?

"Little by little," says Leap, the psychologist.

"We must get going," says Dr. Sody.

Mr. Hap is the forty-sixth patient they have succeeded in releasing.

The Hap family home was pointed out to us by Mrs. Sun's husband.

Mrs. Sun lives in a town called Kampong Kdei, not far away. A while back, the first time we visited her with Dr. Sody, she was thin, with a shaved head, speechless, with no facial expression, and no contact with others. Her husband brought her out of the locked shed that he'd built for her in the bushes behind his tall house. At the time we compared the shed to a box because it had no windows. It could also be compared to a grave. Forty years ago, Mrs. Sun saw a mass grave, right here in the neighborhood, still open at the time. She was pregnant with her fourth child. Seventy-five bodies, all with their throats slit. She gave birth to her fourth child in a state of insanity. That could have triggered her illness, but not caused it—that's what Dr. Sody thinks. So where did the illness come from? The doctor doesn't know. Nor does Mr. Sun. And now he denies what he told us the first time we came: there was no open, mass grave here. His wife didn't see any bodies, he says; he hangs his head and doesn't look us in the eyes. Is he afraid? Of what? Of whom? Did he never imagine we'd be back in a few months, asking about the victims? The people whose spirits, according to the healer, have taken up residence in Mrs. Sun's body? "You heard that from me?" says the old man in surprise, and fixes his gaze on his own bare feet. "Why remember things like that? She never saw any bodies. And she won't come out of the shed today. There's no improvement from the medicine. Well, she maybe shouts less at night. Anyway, I don't know, I've taught myself not to hear her howling. As I've said, she usually lies there naked, locked up. I wasn't expecting you to come by today. Or I would've washed everything with the compressor."

"There won't be any improvement here," Leap tells us quietly.

"We have to keep trying," says Dr. Sody and counts out pills for three months. "Let's go."

We take National Highway 6 north, toward Siem Reap. Slowly. Because before the town of Kampong Kdei ends we turn left at the health center, and rattle down a red road to a junction with another red road. It's around half a mile. Here, opposite a store, there was a naked man lying on a kre—Nel. We haven't seen him for two months. Nel's not here? A few days ago his sister came back from abroad. She's bustling around in the yard. Her brother is lying in the house, still naked. The kre has disappeared from in front of the house.

She and her husband had gone to Thailand, because they had
debts here. They worked on a rubber plantation from 7 A.M. until
5 P.M., for six dollars a day. Whatever they earned, they sent to
their creditors in Cambodia. She fell pregnant, and miscarried.
Then it rained so heavily that the work dried up. They hadn't
put any money aside and came home on borrowed cash. Her
husband? Here, too, there's nothing for him to do. He walks up
and down the red highway, begging, from morning to evening,
and after dark too—it won't end well.

Her brother, Nel? It's a long story. The illness first attacked
him about twenty years ago. The traditional doctor said it was
Muslim black magic. But how on earth? There aren't any Muslims
here. Maybe they were in Phnom Penh? Nel had gone there,
and came home, his head shaved. He told the neighbors some
soldiers had beaten and electrocuted him; it's possible, because
the country wasn't at peace yet then. Young and handsome, he
was walking along, when he ran into some people, hell knows
who they were, maybe they accused him of being a stray black
shirt. There were plenty of those roaming along the roads. Or
vice versa: maybe some of Pol Pot's men saw him as a supporter
of the new authorities, and tortured him. His sister isn't sure
of anything. Maybe the electrocution caused him to think too
much? Or feel too much? He came back strange, aggressive, he
hit everyone. They took him to the healer more than just once
or twice. Black magic? His sister's not sure. Her brother used to
disappear and return. It went on and on, so they had to lock him
up.

Until twenty years later, along came the doctor from Phnom
Penh, gave them the tablets, and he calmed down, he started
talking, he was great. But lately he hasn't been taking the pills

because in his sister's absence their elderly father neglected his treatment. The illness came back. He has lost contact with the world again. But he's not aggressive, nor does he spend the whole time lying down. He gets up, and walks around the village naked, relieving himself wherever. The pills? His sister can't remember how to give them to her brother. Which ones in the morning, which at night? Half or whole? The instructions Dr. Sody wrote on the plastic bag were washed off long ago by the damp. It's lucky she stopped by again today.

"Fetch a bucket of water!"

Dr. Sody is giving orders to people she doesn't know at all. Without ceremony, without a smile. The banana grove has grown thicker, the plastic bottles have risen into piles, the place is now swarming with plastic bags, hanging on the bushes, fluttering. Now we—Dr. Sody, the psychologist, the photographer, and I—are standing behind the small, empty house, and the neighbors are running to us. It's to them that the doctor is giving orders. And she greets the patient, Rean. He no longer looks like Antonio Banderas, but like a large dumpling instead. These drugs increase the appetite, and his aunt doesn't skimp on rice for him. But she evidently skimps on water.

"Will you take a bath?" asks Dr. Sody.

"Sure."

The doctor organizes the washing. One bucket of water isn't enough. Three are needed. Rean picks up a small bowl, and pours water over his head. He soaps up his body.

"Wash yourself all over."

"Okay."

"There too."

"Yes, there too."

"Can we give you a haircut?"

"As long as it looks nice."

"Fetch a pair of scissors!"

And moments later someone brings a pair of heavy tailor's scissors.

"Cut it," Dr. Sody tells the driver. "But nicely."

"And you," she says, addressing the onlookers, "chop back some of those bushes. Let the boy have more light. And take away the trash. It stinks unbearably here."

The neighbors carry out all the orders without a word of protest.

"I've brought you some clothes," says the doctor, handing Rean a brightly colored sarong to cover his hips. And a T-shirt with the TPO logo on it. She helps him get dressed. These are his first clothes in several years. He likes them. There's also a clean hammock to sleep in. The driver and the psychologist take the old one down from the pillars and hang up the new one. But they can't remove the chain of their own accord.

"Thank you," Rean says to the doctor.

"I've brought you some rolls."

"Great."

"Do you like yogurt?"

"Sure."

"It's strawberry."

We watch as he eats it all with relish. He's given a one-liter bottle of water. He drinks it all at once. Then he pees into the empty bottle. And drinks from it again.

"Don't do that," says Dr. Sody, waving a hand. "Do you want more water?"

"Yes."

Finally, the aunt appears. The one who told us a while back about Rean's American wife and their arranged marriage. She doesn't say hello.

"*I am baby*," Rean says to us in English. "I'm two years old."

He's thirty-two. Dr. Sody is satisfied. The patient is clearly taking his pills. It's possible to have a chat with him now. The conversation with the aunt is different today too. "I love that nephew of mine," she says, weeping. "I remember what a great boy he was. Smiling, helpful, clever. I shouldn't love him, I really shouldn't. After all, he killed my sister. I should hate him. That would be right. But I can't. His brothers abandoned him, and I was left alone with him. I have a husband, I have children, and no support or understanding from any of them. He's your Rean, they say, he's yours, not ours. You watch out, or you'll catch it off him. Am I already going crazy?"

"No one would find it easy to be in your shoes," replies the psychologist.

"No one," repeats the doctor.

They seem pleased with the aunt's sensitivity. Next time they'll try to persuade her to remove the chain from her nephew's leg, and untie him from the pillar. It won't be easy. Let's not forget that she chained him up under pressure from the police and the neighbors.

The police station is empty today, as usual. The neighbors are standing outside it, in a wide circle. "Rean is sick," the psychologist explains to them. "We call his illness schizophrenia. Does he talk to himself sometimes? Does he talk nonsense? Does he seem to see someone beside him? It's not evil spirits that have strayed here from the jungle. It's not a curse, or black magic. It's the product of a sick mind. We have to try to cure it. We have the right drugs. When he was ill, Rean was a danger to you, but if he keeps taking the pills, he'll change. You can see he's better already. He's talking, laughing. It's not the person that's dangerous, it's the illness. And that's rare, anyway, because most people with schizophrenia are no threat to anyone, and there's no reason to be afraid of them. Rean is returning to the world of the healthy. That's what we're hoping. Though we can never be certain, because each patient falls sick and recovers in his own way. Rean is going to be fine. But in addition to our medicines, he could do with a bit of human respect, a bit of your company. Drop in on him now and then, so he doesn't just have a lonely life behind the house. Don't make fun of him. You're a community. And he belongs to it. Just as he is. And he's a nice guy, you know that better than I do. Take him some water, water doesn't cost much."

The neighbors are nodding. Maybe they will visit him behind the empty house, maybe they won't, we don't know. Nobody mentions the chain on the sick man's leg. Isn't anyone bothered by it? Does the idea of releasing Rean occur to anyone? "Not yet," replies the psychologist, and listens to what the villagers have to say. But they—there are more and more of them here—are not interested in Rean's illness. As if he weren't part of the life of their village at all. As if they felt no neighborly duty toward the manacled man. They talk about themselves. One of them has heart pain, another has headaches, another one asks about insomnia. In reply to that, the psychologist says there can be three causes: physical, mental, and abuse of harmful substances. He expands on each of these three points in a few sentences, and ends with a joke. They're all laughing. "Laugh, do," he says to the assembled company, "with Rean's aunt, too. Do you ever think of her? She goes around feeling sad. Sadness isn't a good thing. Give her a little joy. We build temples for the Buddha, but we forget that according to his teachings, it's important to help sad people too."

Psychoeducation and a sermon all in one. Leap, the psychologist, is the son of a Buddhist monk. And the father of two children. Although he's talkative, in the year we've spent trailing around the entire country together, that's all he has told us about himself. At the end of the working day, each of us goes to our own room at the hotel. The psychologist, Dr. Sody, the driver, and us. Are they having supper? A beer, perhaps? Together, or each one separately? "Let's get some rest," says Leap every evening. "See you tomorrow!"

She won't drink, she won't eat, she can't sleep, she's dying.

That's what we told Dr. Sody a year ago about a woman of over thirty, whom she had never seen. We found her in a place named Thma Puok, in the north of the country, three hundred miles from Phnom Penh. She was going to be a teacher, she was going to get married, but she fell ill. Seven years ago. She has spent the last three chained up in a shed with no front wall. Undiagnosed and untreated. Naked, bald, a living skeleton fueled by the energy of her illness. Her brain doesn't understand that her body must sleep. When aroused, she's noisy and vulgar. She has been known to threaten the children, saying she'll kill them. Before we knew her name, we called her the Bald Singer. Her actual name is Chroep.

The dry season went by, then the rainy season, then another dry season, now it's pouring again, and we're back.

For the fifth time—Chroep greets us and recognizes everyone. She looks us straight in the eyes, confidently, boldly. Dressed in colorful clothes, with a bobbed haircut, and not so thin anymore. She's happy, smiling—and free. And her mother weeps when she sees Dr. Sody getting out of the car. Tears in Cambodia? By now we know that's a rare sight. Because it means emotion: it says, "I am weak, scared, defenseless." Why make things like that public? The less a stranger knows, the better. You must hide your emotions from strangers. From Dr. Sody? Why? Dr. Sody is one of us, she always brings relief and security. That moves the mother. She's grateful to the doctor for her daughter's health. And so is the father. Now he's sitting on a kre underneath the large house, smiling at us. But we haven't really come to like him, because at every previous visit he kept saying there was no question of releasing his daughter. He couldn't accept that the pills would improve her condition. But Chroep wasn't shouting any more, or being provocative or threatening. She was talking more and more rationally, communicating, sleeping, and eating. After so many years the father couldn't get it into his head that she could get better. He was still afraid of her aggression. Afraid of trouble with the neighbors or the police. Today he's not afraid. "Today," he tells us, "I feel peace and happiness."

A year ago, Dr. Sody came here at our request and diagnosed schizophrenia. The treatment began. Some time passed. "Until my father went away to work somewhere," says Chroep. "He was away from home for several days. Meanwhile my mother sat in the shed with me and wept. She said how evil and dreadful I'd been, that I'd torn out my hair and threatened the children, so she'd had to surround me with a fence made of thorny sticks.

She was pleased I was getting better. And as I talked to her, I could tell that I was moving from illness into good health, as if I were crossing a river, a border. And Momma could see that I was coming out of the darkness. She wept, because at last she could talk to her daughter. She added up the sum she and my father had spent over the years on all those doctors, shamans, folk healers, and monks—ten thousand dollars. They'd sold their whole field, so today they have nothing but the house, and they work for strangers. It's a pity I was so unwell, or I'd have told them what I think of their shamans. Momma asked how much of the illness I remember, or whom. Nobody, nothing. I can't remember the folk healers or the monks, or Dr. Sody's first few visits, or the psychologist who apparently talked to the neighbors, or your interpreter. But I do remember you two. Every single meeting, even the first one. To begin with, you stood here, then you sat on the bench. One time you were ready to head out of here, but your car wouldn't start. I was pleased you'd be staying longer. Finally, someone came and fixed the engine. I wished you a safe journey. I asked if you'd be back. I missed you. Then Momma and I talked about your visits, saying that the bald white man had taken pictures of me, and that I'd been happy to pose for him. And the one in glasses hadn't done anything. He just looked, said nothing more often than he asked questions, and made a few notes in his book."

Now we're all laughing. We explain that if we publish the pictures anywhere, the faces of the patients are always obscured or don't show at all.

"I'm well now," replies Chroep. "Before my father came back, Momma undid the padlock, took the chain off my leg, and hid it somewhere."

Needlessly. On his way back, the father met his daughter on the road. "It's high time," he said. "Come and live in the house."

She didn't. She's afraid to live high up on pillars. She prefers being in her shed, close to the ground. Apart from that, everything else has changed. She sleeps well, soundly, from nightfall to cockcrow. She wakes up, brushes her teeth, combs her hair, cooks some rice, feeds the ducks, talks to her parents, cleans the yard, cycles to the store, on the way she laughs with the local children, who like her, and aren't at all afraid of her because she's nicer than the other adults, she always has the time and energy to play with them. What about the neighbors? They talk about her illness: you were dangerous, noisy, and crude, they say. "Let them talk," says Chroep, waving a hand as if shooing away a fly. "I realize I was a lunatic, but I'm trying not to think of myself like that anymore. I'm congratulating myself, because I've come back from a faraway place. And I thank you, too."

Today, in this yard, no one's ashamed of their tears.

"I've never felt so happy in my life," says the mother, sobbing. "I can't compare it with anything. Or express my gratitude. All those years no one supported me, all those years I was alone. I wouldn't wish that sort of isolation on anybody."

In farewell Dr. Sody warns: "You must take the medicine regularly. Otherwise the illness will return."

Sokni.

"I used to go swimming in the river. Every morning I gave the monks some rice. I used to go to school. I knew how to write. I can speak a little English. I had coffee. The mosquitoes bite. The rats roam around. I'm not hungry. Thank you for the water. Thank you for the visit. I want to go out." Every sentence he speaks is separate, divided from the previous one by a silence, and spoken quietly. With a lukewarm smile. We're looking each other in the eyes. He's sitting, we're standing. He's inside, we're outside.

Sokni's prison has been concealed behind his grandmother's house for fifteen years. A rusty cage six-and-a-half feet high, six-and-a-half feet long, and four feet wide, propped on pillars less than two feet above the ground, or rather above what Sokni has been excreting for years. His grandmother's wooden cottage is hidden on the riverbank, in the undergrowth at the end of the road, which doesn't go any farther. It's stuffy, there's no fresh air.

Sokni is over thirty. His grandmother is over eighty. She tells us about her husband again: when his boat full of rice began to sink, he jumped overboard to save it. His head was underwater for too long. In vain they dragged him out, in vain. For six months he never woke up at all. And then he died. Before Pol Pot.

"Maybe it's time to release your grandson?" says Leap, the psychologist, interrupting the old woman. "He's been taking the pills for three years. His condition has improved."

"Not yet," replies the grandmother. "Maybe next year."

"Why wait a few months? What for?"

"It's necessary."

"He won't do anyone any harm. Why keep anyone locked up?"

"It's necessary to wait."

"What if you were to die this year?"

"Me? I might die tomorrow."

"And who will let your grandson out?"

"I don't know."

"He'll die of thirst and hunger in that cage."

"Him? He's strong. He's going to live a long time. And he won't let my soul depart. He'll keep me trapped on earth."

"Do you want to wander around here in the bushes?"

"As a stray evil spirit? Various things could happen."

"Exactly."

"I won't be able to open the cage on my own."

"Shall we open it?"

"I don't know where I've put the keys. I never needed them."

"They're hanging up here. But will they fit? The padlock's rusted. Use a hammer?"

"A hatchet!"

Leap borrows a small ax from the grandmother and strikes the padlock. The cage shakes, and there's ringing in everyone's ears. Sokni interlocks his hands, so hard that his fingers are going white, but he doesn't say a word, he just follows the movements of the hatchet without so much as a blink. But after a short while, Leap gives up. What's to be done? Our driver goes to the car for a wrench and comes back. He grips the padlock with it, and gives it a whack with the ax butt. The sound of metal being struck echoes around the neighborhood. The first blow, the tenth, the fiftieth. The neighbors come running. And Sokni's mom, from god knows where—clearly, she wasn't far away. The padlock is still refusing to give way, the ax keeps landing on it, ten times more, then another five, the driver is in a sweat by now, but finally he succeeds.

We're opening the cage door.

Sokni puts his palms together vertically in a gesture of thanks to everyone in the vicinity. As if freedom were a gift, not a natural state. Sokni is saying thank you for his freedom. He approaches the exit. He puts a foot outside. He's about to place his bare feet on the bare ground, but someone thoughtfully notices that his feet are too soft for that.

Shoes! He needs shoes.

Sokni turns back. He's looking for something in the depths of his prison. In the makeshift bed he finds a pair of beige, plastic flip-flops. And a peaked cap. He doesn't put on the cap. He's coming out again. He steps onto the ground. He puts on the flip-flops. He smiles. And offers us his hand. Strangers. Foreigners from far away. He squeezes our hands tightly. It's his initiative, his need. His first human touch for fifteen years? Because he doesn't offer his hand to his grandmother or his mom. The mom and the grandmother don't touch him or hug him. Only after a while the old woman helps her grandson to remove his shirt, and takes it away to be laundered. She wipes a speck of dirt from his cheek. That's as far as the affection goes.

Sokni is free!

Bewildered, he sits on the kre, lies down, and goes to sleep.

"So, where's Dr. Sody?"

Kim has a disappointed look on his face, because he can see she's not with us.

"She was detained by other duties," explains the psychologist. "She stayed in Phnom Penh."

"I often go to Phnom Penh in my dreams."

"What do you do there?"

"I walk around the colorful streets. I know the city. I sit outside the royal palace. I talk to people. I feed the pigeons. I look at the great river. I have something good to eat at a restaurant. I have my hair cut at a barber's. I laugh. I ride in a tuk-tuk. I buy jeans, shoes, a phone."

"Who do you want to call?"

"My aunt, my grandma, and my grandpa. To tell them how I'm spending my time in the big city."

His aunt, grandmother, and grandfather are all he has in the world. As we know from our last visit, his parents died of AIDS, and his sister went off into the unknown. She left her brother locked up in a walled cell, right beside a noisy highway, with cars racing along it from the capital to the city of Battambang.

The aunt, who keeps him locked up, is not much older than her nephew. Kim is twenty-eight. Skinny, naked, smiling. With psychosis, triggered by methamphetamines. It's been six years since he's taken any, since he was first locked up. The illness should have gone away, but it didn't. Until a year ago, when Dr. Sody came to visit. She brought some medicine. The aunt has been giving it to Kim carefully, regularly, so the patient, formerly uncommunicative, has finally started to talk. But even today he's looking at the world through three barred windows. In between the bars facing the road and the bars facing the house there's a hammock. Under the hammock there's white terracotta tiling. Every day it's swept and washed by the aunt. Or rather it was, because right now the floor is sticky with dirt.

"He asked, he insisted," replies the aunt. "So I opened his cell. Let him live, I thought, because he's talking normally, he's normal, he has to be let out. It's been six months now, since he jumped with joy and danced around, thanking everyone for his freedom. There aren't many of us at home, so he went to the highway to stop the cars. To thank the drivers, everyone in turn. Some people tapped their foreheads—plainly, they couldn't understand him, they didn't know that to some people freedom can matter more than anything else. The days went by, and he went on sleeping in his cell, but it was always open. He didn't resort to drugs, nothing of the kind. But every morning he rode off on his scooter to go on thanking people. He was a bit of a pest at the gas station, but nothing major."

"Some of the people swore at me," says Kim, supplementing his aunt's account, because we're talking in his presence. He's behind the bars, we're in front of them.

"Got any cigarettes?"

"Do you smoke a lot?" asks the psychologist.

"Grandma gives me a pack a day."

"A pack?"

"I smoke the whole pack."

"That's why your teeth are black."

Why is Kim in his cell again? Because when he was freed, he went to a wedding at the neighbors' house. He had a drink. How much did he drink? Nobody was keeping track. He picked up a knife and went for his aunt with it. The men seized him instantly, by the legs, by the arms, dragged him here, and flung him into his cell like a sack of rice.

"It was a dreadful sight," says his aunt today. "He struggled and screamed, he regretted it and apologized. Am I afraid to wash the floor since then? No way! Nothing much happened. I'd let him out again. He's been back inside for two months now. But his grandmother won't allow it."

The grandmother is looking at us as if we weren't beside her at all. She says nothing, just smokes one cigarette after another.

"Are you going to let him out?" the psychologist asks her.

"Maybe one day." These are her first words.

"When?"

"In a while."

"He'll be well-behaved."

"Not now."

At this, a white-haired man gets up from a kre. He's been listening in on our conversation from the start. He hasn't said a word. A snooping neighbor? No, he's Kim's grandfather. "Why not now?" he asks, and removes the wire from the staple that serves as a padlock.

Kim bolts out, smiling, and greets each of us, grabbing each one by the arms for a few seconds. His grandfather, his grandmother, his aunt, and us. "Okun," he keeps saying. "Okun! Thank you!"

He runs to the pots, and picks up a lid, there can't be anything in it, but he's not disheartened. Once again, he runs up to everyone in turn, touches each person in turn, and embraces them. "Okun! Okun! Okun!"

"Go," says his grandmother, fending off her grandson's hugs. And with a smile she gives him three crumpled banknotes. "Buy yourself something to eat."

Kim mounts his scooter. He rides off.

Black blood beneath her toes?

Last time there wasn't any blood. Or any communication with the patient who killed her father. It's Sinuon. Her eyes were immobile and glassy, but alive. Emaciated, naked. Dr. Sody gave her some rolls and a bottle of water. She brought new medicine, because the old pills had gone missing. She left them with the two aunts—sisters of the girl's dead mother.

According to the aunts, it happened like this: the girl's father brought her some bananas. He divided the bunch in two, to share it between his daughter and his grandson. Sinuon ate all hers, and then said to her son: "Give me some more." The boy grabbed his bananas and ran off. The mother went after him. With a knife. The grandfather saw this, and ran to protect his grandson. The five-year-old watched as his mother stabbed his grandfather eighteen times.

"She was like a tiger," the aunts tell us.

"Let's start from the beginning," says Dr. Sody. "Sinuon went away to Phnom Penh, and after a while she came home in an altered state. Aggressive, so her father locked her up. Just after her mother's death. She spent a year living on a chain, here beneath the house, until someone told us about her. We came to help. After three months of treatment, her father undid the chain. Because she had improved. We were satisfied. She even went to work. To the town, nearby. She collected trash from the street, bits of plastic, and cabbage leaves at the market. That put her father off his guard. He neglected her treatment, which we didn't find out about in time. The daughter's illness returned instantly. And she killed her father.

"You can't escape a tiger," the aunts tell us. "Eighteen blows."

The police came, but they didn't take the killer away. The court refrained from imposing a punishment. They gave orders for her to be imprisoned here. So the aunts locked her up, as her father had done previously, beneath the floor of the house. A wooden house, let's be reminded, standing on twelve concrete pillars.

The aunts live in the neighborhood. They bring the prisoner a bowl of rice once a day. They take care of her child. What about the sick girl's sisters, the two who work as seamstresses in Phnom Penh? They haven't dropped by for ages, they haven't sent a penny.

After the father's death, Dr. Sody came to see the patient again, and brought some new medicine. Sinuon has been taking it for a few months now. How does she feel today? "Bad," she tells us herself. "Give me the money for some medicine."

She shows us her mutilated feet. It's dark, fresh blood, slimy with pus. What happened? She doesn't answer. But her aunts know: she kicks the concrete pillar to which she's chained. As if trying to rip off her entire foot. So now she has a chain on her hands too, an extra one to make sure she can't break free. The village would never forgive that.

It's not the patient we can hear groaning, it's Dr. Sody—she's sighing, and shaking her head, because she can't find the words to express her refusal to accept what she's seeing.

The village is afraid of the madwoman. For example, the young tailor in the house next door. That day, she was sitting at her sewing machine, when she heard a noise, as if something had been smashed on the other side of the fence, a large clay pot, perhaps, or something else, but definitely bigger than a glass. Then minutes later she saw the mad Sinuon at her gate, holding a knife from which blood was dripping onto the red road. "That crazy woman should be taken away somewhere," says the neighbor. "We have children here. She screams day and night. She's always reeling off names."

Whose names? All the names she knows. She calls on the living and the dead, as if wanting to be in a crowd. But she's all alone, under her father's house, day and night, among undergrowth that grows ever greener, ever thicker, making her less and less visible to the village. But the village is perfectly well aware that she's here. The parricide. An evil woman. She tried to kill her own child with a knife. Might the village do her harm? "That would put an end to it," says the neighbor, "but everyone's afraid to go near her. They're afraid of the empty house above her head. It's an evil house, an evil place, evil spirits."

So maybe it's a good thing the two seamstress sisters still haven't conducted the mourning ceremony? The second, more important one? Maybe the result is that Sinuon is still safe. The nocturnal spirits are protecting her. The hundredth day since her father's death passed long ago. A sudden and unnatural end demands some special, extra rituals, but the two sisters haven't even seen to the basic ones. They're breaking the moral code. The murder victim's soul is refusing to go away, it's roaming the local homes, it's restless, it's getting angrier. That's for sure: Sinuon's father has already paid a visit to almost all the neighbors as they sleep. "Kmouch chhar," says the young tailor.

That means "a not stewed ghost," we're told.

Not stewed? "Uncooked," says the interpreter instead. Raw? Maybe more like unprepared? Not ready for the journey. Lost. Hungry. Annoyed by the long wait. The whole of Cambodia is teeming with spirits that aren't ready for their journey. People see them standing at crossroads, on the roadside, at the sites of accidents. And in the killing fields from the days of Pol Pot. The country is full of killing fields. They're inhabited by spirits, thousands of them, whole crowds, swarms of spirits whose reincarnation cannot be completed. Ghosts of the past. The living are constantly aware of their company, and they're afraid of them.

There's only one person in the village who isn't afraid of anything. Neither hungry ghosts, nor people. He wears a ring on his leg too. An initiation ring. One time he went crazy after drinking too much, his mother locked him up, and those people from Phnom Penh released him. The ring on his ankle is a weapon to deal with drunks. The local drinkers shouldn't encourage him to misbehave. But they do. He doesn't give in. He doesn't drink. He alone has sympathy for Sinuon, he alone listens to her. She talks to him. About what? About whom? About her beloved husband: he used to hit her, and then he left her.

Others have words of contempt for Sinuon: nutjob, loony, fuck-up, bitch, whore, junkie, murderer. We know this from her aunts and from the neighbors. A person like her isn't fed, or given medical treatment—a person like that should die. The aunts do bring her food, though not much, and they give her the pills, because that's what their sister would have wanted, the sick girl's mother. What do they feel for their niece?

"She just shits and pisses," they say. "Pisses and shits."

What sort of future is there for her? The aunts look around hesitantly. They're both surprised by this obvious question, as if each is expecting some sort of hint from the other. "She'll hear roosters in the morning," says the older one at last. "And dogs at night," adds the younger. And then what? Then she'll die. She won't realize she has died. She'll remain under her father's house, but the chain will come off. She'll roam among the houses, hungry. Would she be happy to chat with the neighbors, with her aunts, and her son? To sit here, then over there, on first one kre, then the next one, free at last, conscious at last? No, instead she'll be insatiable, furious, vengeful. She'll haunt everyone in turn at night. They'll wake up in terror. Then her older sisters will come from Phnom Penh, so they predict, and together with the aunts they'll hold some expensive ceremonies in the village. They'll wish the dead girl a safe journey to heaven. Maybe two ceremonies won't be enough, maybe the monks will say they have to repeat the rituals. And they'll repeat them. It would be good to have it all behind them by now. To be able to purge the house of evil spirits. The monks will help with that too. The sisters will put the house up for sale. But first, she has to die on that chain. There's no hope for someone who has killed her own father.

ACKNOWLEDGEMENTS AND MORE

I'd been wanting to write about Cambodia for a long time, since 2002, when my book about post-war Bosnia, *Like Eating A Stone*,[1] was first published. Before that, while working in Sarajevo and Srebrenica, I had read a lot about genocide. The knowledge gained gave me a better understanding of how and why it happens. But it didn't answer the most important questions: how, after mass killing, are the perpetrators and the survivors able to live together, at close quarters? In a single country, in a single city, in a single village, at the same firm or school? And sometimes inside a single body. In Bosnia, at least at that time, soon after the war, the answer seemed clear: they can't do it. They have to live in a world that's split in half—there's no other way.

But the examples of Cambodia and Rwanda, which at that point I only knew from the media and literature, showed that the survivors of genocide have no choice. They have to live alongside the murderers. What is life like under those conditions? I had no idea. I couldn't imagine it. And when a reporter has no idea, and can't find the answer in the available literature to a question

---

[1] Wojciech Tochman, *Like Eating A Stone: Surviving the Past in Bosnia*, translated by Antonia Lloyd-Jones, Atlas & Co, 2008.

that's bothering him, he has to board a train or a plane, reach the relevant place and make an effort to seek it on the spot.

At first, traveling to Cambodia was beyond my capacities in every regard. Perhaps it would be more honest to say that Cambodia terrified me. Of course, I did know that the Khmer Rouge and the Khmers were not the same thing, but I couldn't shake off my fear of setting foot behind the former bamboo curtain. The land of the Khmers was like a dark chasm. But I persuaded myself I was interested in that darkness, and that there was nothing extraordinary, suspicious, or perverse about my interests. Darkness is the reporter's natural environment. The brightly lit world is not a topic for him.

I flew to South-East Asia for the first time two months after *Like Eating A Stone* was published. Not to Cambodia, but to the Indonesian island of Bali, where on October 12, 2002, the Polish reporter Beata Pawlak was killed in a terrorist attack. At first we had no information about her death, just that she was missing. I flew there to look for her. The bad news was confirmed a few weeks later. I went back to Poland, and a year later I returned to Bali. I settled there for a while to do the research for a report on Beata, who had been writing about terrorism when she was murdered by terrorists on this idyllic island. I wrote a book titled *Dear Daughter*.[2] The subject was important, but the book was weak, as I only realized after it came out, unfortunately. Trying to find an excuse, I told myself that while Asia is very beautiful, it's not my professional terrain. I don't understand Asia. Today, I have a different take on that particular failure, but this isn't the place to elaborate.

---

[2] Tochman, *Córeńka* [Dear Daughter], Społeczny Instytut Wydawniczy Znak, 2005.

Finally, several years later, while on vacation in Thailand, I decided that as Cambodia was just across the border, I'd fly to Phnom Penh for a three-day reconnaissance trip. I landed at a small, sun-scorched airport. Those sheds probably don't exist anymore, or at least they don't serve passengers. Nowadays the capital city boasts a new terminal, with a Starbucks and lots of plate-glass windows. But that was the hot August of 2007. I rode in a tuk-tuk to Monivong Boulevard, one of the main avenues, to the Asia Hotel. My small, bright room had a broken window. So I slept with the clamor of the city, and with a puddle on the floor, because it always rained at night. I went to the suburbs to see the killing fields, and visited Tuol Sleng prison in the city center. I watched the people. They were smiling.

Should I come back here? Write a book? Everything about this noisy, bright, low-rise city seemed to me distant, inaccessible, incomprehensible. Above all, the people. They were cordial enough, but reserved. On top of that, a resident of Phnom Penh who showed me the city, a musician and college tutor, strongly discouraged me. With a smile on his face he foretold difficulties and restrictions: to work in Cambodia I would have to have accreditation, and employ an interpreter assigned to me by the government. For a government fee. I couldn't agree to that—to any reporter it's obvious that working with a government informer would make no sense.

I humbly concluded it wasn't that they were closed-off; it was that I couldn't (yet?) find the space inside myself to tackle their rather recent pain. Or to face up to Asia. Did I drop it? Give up? I certainly doubted I'd manage to identify and understand the issues of interest to me there well enough to write a book about them.

In search of the answers to my important questions I flew
to Africa. To Rwanda, where in 1994 a million people had been
massacred. There—thanks to contacts given to me in Poland by
Father Adam Boniecki—right from the start, the glass wall sep-
arating me from reality felt thinner. And indeed, I quite quickly
succeeded in breaking it. I flew regularly from Warsaw to Kigali
for the next two years, until in 2010 *Today We'll Draw Death*[3]
was published, the second of the three books I planned to write
about how life goes on after genocide.

During my work on *Today We'll Draw Death* I also made
some trips to Cambodia. I went there once or twice a year,
beyond the capital now, off the tourist trail. The more I saw,
the less I understood, and the more convinced I became that I
wouldn't be able to tell the story of the Khmers. There won't be a
third book, I thought, it's just not my part of the world.

Exhausted by my experiences in Rwanda, at home in Warsaw
I occupied myself with establishing the Reportage Institute
Foundation and a café-bookstore specializing in reportage. It
took me some time. There, in November 2011, I was sitting on
a windowsill drinking coffee, when on my computer screen I
saw some photographs from the Philippines, taken by Grzegorz
Wełnicki. We met a day or two later, and soon after we flew
to Manila together. I mention it here, because it was thanks
to Grzegorz that I had the courage to write about Asia for the
first time since Bali. In the Philippines, I saw that Asia isn't
such a closed book to us at all, not as inscrutable, and that I
could actually understand some of it, get a sense of it. Two years

[3] Tochman, *Dzisiaj narysujemy śmierć* [Today We'll Draw Death],
Wydawnictwo Czarne, 2010.

later, my book *Eli, Eli*[4] was published, about life in the slums of Manila.

And then I spent another two years traveling around South-East Asia with Grzegorz. These were not planned trips, but spontaneous encounters whenever our paths crossed somewhere on the Red River or the Mekong. Then we would work together for three days, sometimes a week, or a month. Thanks to Grzegorz, I wrote my first short reports from Vietnam, Laos, and Cambodia.

Here and there in *Roosters Crow* . . . I mention the photographer. In fact, this refers to two different people. The first one is Grzegorz Wełnicki, a great pal, superb at his art. It was with him that I found the abandoned teenager who weighed people and played the gong chime. It was with Grzegorz that I visited the Magic Boy who healed people. In Siem Reap we accompanied the bookseller Teng Dara at work. And outside Battambang we talked to the inhabitants of the village of Roka about their mass infection with HIV. We also made a joint effort to have a conversation with "the man who photographed the moment before the end." These stories appeared in a different shape in the Polish monthly magazines *Kontynenty* and *Duży Format* in 2014 and 2015. Some of them were illustrated by Grzegorz's photographs.

The stories about Teng Dara and about the people infected with HIV were published in 2015 as an introduction to the second edition of Zbigniew Domarańczyk's book *Kampuchea, Zero Hour*.[5] The first edition, issued in 1982, stood on the

---

[4] Tochman, *Eli Eli* [Eli, Eli], Wydawnictwo Czarne, 2013.

[5] Zbigniew Domarańczyk, *Kampucza, godzina zero* [Kampuchea, Zero Hour], Dowody na istnienie, 2015.

bookshelf in my parents' sitting room, so I read it when I was fourteen years old. And finally found out who Pol Pot was, because I was familiar with the name before then, if only from the television news. It was Domarańczyk, a Pole, who was the first foreign journalist to enter Cambodia after the fall of the Khmer Rouge dictatorship in January 1979. Not the famous Italian Tiziano Terzani, who claimed to have received Visa Number One at the embassy in Hanoi. Domarańczyk's testimony covers an extraordinary range, which as a teenager I wasn't fully able to appreciate. But at the time I certainly memorized plenty of interesting details, such as the fact that in June the Mekong river stops moving in front of the royal palace, then rises, and a few days later reverses its flow.

In 2016, during one my successive trips to Phnom Penh, I learned about the slum in the old movie house. I went there briefly to get to know the terrain, and it occurred to me that perhaps this could be the subject of my book. My initial plan was that each family living in the movie house, each room, each shack, would provide me with a story, each one on a different topic, happening now, but going a long way back in time. A summary of fortunes, gathered in that place, where the mound stinking of corpses keeps rising, would form a picture of today's Cambodia, living in the shadow of genocide. I explained my idea to Lidia Ostałowska, the eminent reporter who was a close friend of mine. Lidia had doubts: a movie house, a slum, it could be interesting, but is it enough for a book? "Give it a try," she said. "You can always change your mind."

To research my previous books, I had flown from Warsaw to Sarajevo, Kigali, and Manila, spending a few weeks in each place before coming home, and then after a while I'd set off again. I called the time spent in Poland the book's ripening stage. But I realized that in the case of Cambodia, this sort of working rhythm wouldn't pass the test. I knew I had to live there almost permanently, to get to grips with everyday life there, and maybe then I'd be ready to write a book. Or finally admit defeat.

In January 2017, I flew to Phnom Penh and rented an apartment not far from the Boeung Keng Kang market on Street 398. Research topic: the old movie house in Riverside.

By then my invaluable companion was Michał Fiałkowski, whom I had met in Cambodia some time earlier. He took the cover photo and the photos included in this book. Michał and I went to the old movie house together. When I stopped at the entrance to the main auditorium, dark as a cave, Michał went inside first. That's often what happened. It was Michał who blazed the trail, with me behind him. Together we documented the demise of the White Building. The photograph that opens the middle section of this book ("Broken Courage Syndrome") was taken at this historic building's final hour—when everyone moved out.

During our research at the brick factories we were anxious, because not everyone was happy for us to be there. We spent many consecutive days visiting it to research the subject as thoroughly as we could. Michał has pictures that document the labor performed by children and their everyday existence in life-threatening conditions. Michał came with me to Takeo, to visit the prosthetic limb factory and the nearby killing field. We were also together when we talked to the women living over water topped with a concrete platform, and then to the four old ladies forced by their families to beg on the sun-scorched highway leading to the zoo.

We were helped by both male and female interpreters, who translated our conversations from Khmer into English. These were people of various ages, and with various levels of education, including a teacher of Khmer, a teacher of English, and sometimes a teacher of French. There were also some guides to the Angkor temples, some motorbike taxi drivers, and tuk-tuk drivers. After a week or two, each of our interpreters found a way out of any further collaboration. They said they had family problems, or they simply didn't turn up the next day. At first, Michał and I couldn't understand what was wrong. They'd received fair payment, and there hadn't been any quarrels between us—on the contrary, we thought everything was fine, and everyone was happy. Finally, after some of them unfriended us on Facebook, someone explained to us that it was to do with fear. In their first few days of working for us, the interpreters would have realized we were touching on political issues. The old movie house, the White Building, the concrete platform for the outcasts, the brick factories, accidents on construction sites, and everyday violence—all of that is political. And people in Cambodia are afraid of politics. Especially as we were there in the time leading up to an election, when Prime Minister Hun Sen was brutally crushing the opposition, and intimidating everyone in the process. So I had to give up on a few topics. For example, the construction of dams on the rivers, which involves flooding villages and forced displacement. Nobody was willing to go there with us.

My sincere thanks to my interpreters. All of them, without exception, made every effort to help me as best they could. I highly appreciate their work. I won't give their names here, because I wouldn't want them to be at risk of any unpleasantness because of my book. One of them, who lives in Siem Reap, deserves my particular thanks, for supporting my work in a special way. He is old enough to remember the Khmer Rouge very well, and he understands a great deal. We first met in 2014, when on the way to Pol Pot's grave, in the far north of the country, he explained some issues to me that I found incomprehensible. And recently, while I was writing this book, we talked at length about Khmer spirituality, Khmer Buddhism, beliefs, and customs.

On the topic of beliefs, an invaluable source was *Spirit Worlds*[6] by Philip Coggan, an Australian journalist who lived in Cambodia. It was in his work that I found organized information about the flying head, the *arp*. But also the detail about the firefighters who will only put out a house fire if paid a bribe in advance.

While I was writing *Roosters Crow, Dogs Cry*, in the run-up to the election, the authorities closed down *The Cambodia Daily*, one of the two English-language newspapers published in Phnom Penh, citing tax irregularities. I would like to express my respect for its journalists, and my immense gratitude to them. Also to my colleagues at *The Phnom Penh Post*, which for the time being is still being published. Their journalism is not just proof of daily courage, but also an example of great professionalism. I began every working day in Cambodia by reading these two newspapers, which were always interesting. The information I found on their pages prompted me to follow up on certain matters with some first-hand research of my own. These included the mass HIV infection in the village of Roka, and the slave labor at the brick factories.

---

[6] Philip Coggan, *Spirit Worlds: Cambodia, the Buddha & the Naga*, John Beaufoy Publishing 2015.

It was in *The Phnom Penh Post* that one day I read a short interview with a psychiatrist named Sotheara Chhim, who heads the Transcultural Psychosocial Organization (TPO). He talked about the mentally sick people who are kept prisoner by their own families. I was moved, but also surprised, because after a quick check online I found out that no journalist had ever written a book about these people's tragedy. I sent the doctor an email asking if we could meet. We had our first conversation in March 2017. The doctor thought we'd be done after one meeting, but instead there were lots of them. For the chapter titled "*Baksbat*," I also used several of Sotheara Chhim's academic papers. I'll mention two of them here. The first one is "*Baksbat* (Broken Courage): A Trauma-Based Cultural Syndrome in Cambodia," published in *Medical Anthropology*[7], and the second is "A Place for *Baksbat* (Broken Courage) in Forensic Psychiatry at the Extraordinary Chambers in the Courts of Cambodia (ECCC), published in *Psychiatry, Psychology and Law*.[8]

Dr. Sotheara introduced us to the psychiatric doctor and the psychologist who bring the captive patients medical aid. Dr. Ang Sody (whose picture opens this part of the book) and psychologist Seang Leap are big-hearted professionals, as we were able to see for ourselves in the course of our numerous joint expeditions. I am extremely grateful to Dr. Sody and to Leap for inviting us to work with them, for the confidence they placed in Michał and

---

[7] Sotheara Chhim, "*Baksbat* (Broken Courage): A Trauma-Based Cultural syndrome in Cambodia," *Medical Anthropology: Cross-Cultural Studies in Health and Illness*, Volume 32, 2013, issue 2 pages 160-73.

[8] Chhim, "A Place for *Baksbat* (Broken Courage) in Forensic Psychiatry at the Extraordinary Chambers in the Courts of Cambodia (ECCC)," *Psychiatry, Psychology and Law*, Volume 21, 2014, issue 2, pages 286-296.

me, and for their patience. I am also grateful to the other specialists from TPO headquarters and at the unit in Battambang, who helped me to document the drama of the captive patients. My thanks are also due to the TPO drivers, Duong Chiva and Sok Kosal, thanks to whom we always reached our remote and sometimes inaccessible destinations safely, and usually on time.

We made our trips to see the patients between June 2017 and August 2018. I have described most of them in this book. As I have stressed, on some occasions we accompanied the TPO. These visits did not usually last long, an hour or less, because we had to drive on, to visit the next patients. And so I went to see all the people I have described again, either once or several times, without the doctor and the psychologist. This allowed me—with the help of an interpreter—to have an unhurried conversation with the families, the neighbors, and finally with the patients themselves. I was almost always accompanied by Michał Fiałkowski. There are pictures of all of the patients in his archive. Whenever he publishes any of these photos, he always preserves their anonymity: the faces are not recognizable, and in my text I only give their first names. I made two trips to visit patients accompanied by two other photographers, Anna Liezl Natalicio and Mariusz Grabowski.

My special thanks are due to Ewa Jankowska, owner of the wonderful Pelikan, a Polish pierogi bar in Phnom Penh. Entirely disinterestedly, but with patience and great sensitivity, Ewa interpreted for me during my conversation with Nhep Sary, the teacher and heroine of the chapter titled "The year of all the deaths." Altogether, we had seven meetings at Mrs. Sary's house.

At the time, there was a small group of Poles living in Phnom Penh. They too helped me to research the book: the architect

Paweł Siudecki, the musician Marcin Maciejewski, and Paweł Bólek, living in Takeo, who probably knows all there is to know about Khmer customs.

I'd like to add a few notes about my background reading. Over eleven years of spending time in Cambodia, I read dozens of reports, books by journalists, essays, monographs, and historical works. One of the titles to which I often returned while writing *Roosters Crow, Dogs Cry* was *Cambodia Now: Life in the Wake of War* by Karen J. Coates.[9] I bought it at a bookstore in Phnom Penh in 2007, and soon found it to be an extraordinary work of reportage. From 1998 (when Pol Pot died), the author worked at *The Cambodia Daily*, and got to know the country extremely well. It was in her book that I first read about the trauma left behind by the Khmer Rouge genocide, and how people try to cope with it. Here too I first came upon the name of Dr. Ang Sody: she was already a psychiatrist, but wasn't yet working for the TPO. And this is where I first read about the TPO, at a time when its employees didn't yet know they would be helping captive patients.

I frequently went back to Philip Short's monumental biography, *Pol Pot: Anatomy of a Nightmare*, published in 2004.[10] It's a mine of information that enabled me to understand numerous issues and processes. I sourced many details from it, for the most part cited in Dr. Sody's back story, including facts about the date of the last river convoy to have sailed into the besieged capital with food, about the amounts of ammunition

---

[9] Karen J. Coates, *Cambodia Now: Life in the Wake of War*, McFarland & Co, 2005.

[10] Philip Short, *Pol Pot: Anatomy of a Nightmare*, Henry Holt & Company 2005.

and food supplied by air drops, and about how, on entering Phnom Penh, Pol Pot's young guerrillas drank the water from toilet bowls and ate toothpaste. Another detail that I found in Short's book concerned the number of patients forced to leave the hospital and get out of Phnom Penh.

I was also accompanied by *Cambodia* by Adam W. Jelonek.[11] This is an excellent analysis of the Khmer genocide, in which I found many useful details, for instance the information about the total weight of bombs dropped on Cambodia by American bombers.

And Tiziano Terzani, a major author of many books, witness to the most tragic events in the twentieth-century history of the Indochinese Peninsula. He saw at close hand not just the Vietnam war, but also the consequences of the American bombing of Cambodia. In April 1975, only days after the Khmer Rouge entered Phnom Penh, Terzani was assigned the task of a "carrier pigeon"—each week, one of the correspondents working there collected his colleagues' dispatches and flew to Bangkok, from where he sent them abroad by telex. This time the return journey proved impossible, because the planes had stopped flying to Phnom Penh. Terzani tried to cross the land border into Cambodia, but was very nearly killed, and went back to Thailand. There, for the next few years he gathered the accounts of survivors who had managed to escape from behind the bamboo curtain.

While living and working in Phnom Penh, I sometimes used to relax on the terrace of the legendary Foreign Correspondents Club, where I'd grab a cold drink and watch the Mekong as it

---

[11] Adam W. Jelonek, *Kambodża* [Cambodia], Wydawnictwo Trio, 2008.

merged with the Tonlé Sap, and think about the chroniclers of those past events. Let's remember the most important names: the American Sydney Schanberg (who died in 2016) and his interpreter Dith Pran (who died in 2008)—we know their story from the British movie, *The Killing Fields*, based on Schanberg's book, *The Death and Life of Dith Pran*.[12] He must have been acquainted with Koki Ishihara, the journalist and Japanese translator of Orwell, who before the fall of Phnom Penh set off into territory occupied by the Khmer Rouge. He never came back. I'd like to write about him one day. And about Tiziano Terzani. He worked for the Italian press, and also the German weekly, *Der Spiegel*. His articles were collected and published after his death in 2004 into a single volume titled *Ghosts: Dispatches from Cambodia*.[13] I have never been a great fan of Terzani's work, and have always felt the comparison between him and Ryszard Kapuściński to be a gross exaggeration. But his books are full of details of everyday life from both before and after the genocide, for which I value them. I learned from Terzani how much rice could be bought for a doctor's salary, how many doctors there were in Cambodia before Pol Pot, and how many were left after him. So his *Ghosts* . . . was an important source of information for me.

I would like to thank all my consultants.

The psychologists at the Wrocław SWPS (University of Social Sciences and Humanities), including psychotherapist Katarzyna Kossobudzka and Professor Justyna Ziółkowska, and also the Warsaw-based psychiatrist Dr. Maciej Kopera each read

[12] Sydney Schanberg, *The Death and Life of Dith Pran*, Penguin, 1980.

[13] Tiziano Terzani, *Fantasmi: dispacci dalla Cambogia* [Ghosts: Dispatches from Cambodia], Longanesi & Co, 2008.

through a draft computer file, and then shared their questions and doubts with me. Their critical comments had a vital effect on the shape of the text, and also drew my attention to some linguistic pitfalls involving words that are no longer appropriate. However, one of them, "retarded," does appear in the book, in a comment by Dr. Sody, which I decided to quote without change.

The first draft of the completed manuscript was read by Professor Piotr Ostaszewski, an expert on Cambodia, whom I thank for drawing my attention to several points, including a very basic one: the number of victims of the 1975-1979 genocide. Different sources give different data. In Professor Ostaszewski's view, the most reliable figures range from 900,000 to 1,100,000. As a result, this book mentions a million victims. This number should be regarded as approximate, and to it should be added the around half a million killed in the Cambodian Civil War of 1970-1975, plus another half million who died as a result of famine after January 1979.

What would Lidia Ostałowska have said about *Roosters Crow, Dogs Cry* ? Her death, in January 2018, found me working on the chapter about the women who'd been evicted from the city. Lidia always wrote about the weakest people, so I believe this book would have met with her approval. But every single phrase? I don't think so, although I tried to keep watch as I wrote. Whenever I felt that my descriptions were becoming too baroque, I glanced at a picture of Lidia, and immediately sensed what she would have said about that sort of writing. Thanks to her gaze, many words were expelled from this book without mercy.

Iza Klementowska helped me with the statistics cited in the chapter about the old movie house, and also gave me some no-nonsense comments after reading a draft. Thanks to Iza's powers of observation I was able to avoid a certain opinion that was founded on stereotype.

Katarzyna Boni had a major influence on the structure; despite pressing work on her own book she found the time to read mine several times, prompting me to rethink several themes, and raising my spirits at moments of doubt. The first readers of the finished book included Beata Chmiel and Ewa Wanat, and thanks to the green light they gave me, I dared to send the manuscript to Wydawnictwo Literackie publishing house, which in 2017 adopted me, along with my previous publications too. Thank you.

Thank you to Magdalena Petryńska, editor of this book as well as my earlier works, for her professionalism and for having the patience of a saint.

Lots of clever people contributed to the work on *Roosters Crow, Dogs Cry* and they did a superb job. But for the final shape of the text, and thus for any remaining errors, I alone bear the responsibility.

Finally, my most special words of gratitude are reserved for the heroes of this book. Thank you to all the friendly people I have met in Cambodia over the years, whether at the old movie house in downtown Phnom Penh, or in some remote place far from the highway, far from everything, such as the Magic Boy's village, or the village of Roka. Some of the people who feature in the book appear by name, while for various reasons others remain anonymous. I am grateful to them all for their stories, most of which were not easy to tell, and also for the trust that did in fact prove possible between us. Without that trust I could never have written this book. I hope I haven't offended anyone; I certainly never intended to. The only people who talk about the Khmers in this book are Khmers themselves. I merely pose the questions, and ask the Khmers to explain the things I cannot understand.

I am extremely grateful to everyone I met in Cambodia who was suffering from mental illness, and to their families too, though they will probably never read *Roosters Crow, Dogs Cry* Neither Talan, whose picture in the cage opens the first part of the book ("Operation Unchain"), nor Rean, who is washing himself in the picture that opens the third part. I'd like to stress that their fate is close to my heart. I believe they could sense that. As I've mentioned in the book, there's never enough money to treat the captive patients. The Cambodian government ignores the issue. But there is the TPO, which I know to be a fully reliable organization. In the hope that my readers will be interested in supporting Operation Unchain, I would like to refer them to the TPO's website (https://tpocambodia.org/), or to the Global Giving site where it's possible to make a donation: https://www.globalgiving.org/donate/28727/cambodia-trans-cultural-psychosocial-organization/, or to the Polish foundation, Klub Heban: https://www.facebook.com/KlubHeban/. Thank you very much. I am convinced that the help Dr. Sody can give her patients will restore their liberty and bring an end to their suffering.

December 2018

WOJCIECH TOCHMAN (b. 1969) is one of Poland's bestknown authors of literary non-fiction. His published works include *Like Eating a Stone* and *Today We'll Draw Death*, which together with *Roosters Crow, Dogs Cry* form a triptych about everyday life following genocide in, respectively, Bosnia Herzegovina, Rwanda and Cambodia. His books have been translated into a large number of European languages. He has won numerous prizes including the Premio Kapuscinski awarded in Rome. For the past few years he has been living in Greece.

ANTONIA LLOYD-JONES has translated works by many of Poland's leading contemporary novelists, including Nobel Prize winner Olga Tokarczuk, Jacek Dehnel, Mariusz Szczygieł, and Artur Domosławski. She has been a mentor for the Emerging Translator Mentorship Program and co-chair of the UK Translators Association. In 2018 she was honored with Poland's Transatlantyk Award for the most outstanding promoter of Polish literature abroad.

**OPEN
LETTER**

OPEN LETTER

**OPEN
LETTER**

Kjersti A. Skomsvold (Norway)
The Child
Andrzej Sosnowski (Poland)
Lodgings
Albena Stambolova (Bulgaria)
Everything Happens as It Does
Benjamin Stein (Germany)
The Canvas
Georgi Tenev (Bulgaria)
Party Headquarters
Dubravka Ugresic (Europe)
The Age of Skin
American Fictionary
Europe in Sepia
Fox
Karaoke Culture
Nobody's Home
Thank You for Not Reading
Ludvík Vaculík (Czech Republic)
The Guinea Pigs
Antoine Volodine (France)
Bardo or Not Bardo
Post-Exoticism in Ten Lessons,
*   Lesson Eleven*
Radiant Terminus
Jorge Volpi (Mexico)
Season of Ash
Eliot Weinberger (ed.) (World)
Elsewhere
Ingrid Winterbach (South Africa)
The Book of Happenstance
The Elusive Moth
To Hell with Cronjé
Ror Wolf (Germany)
Two or Three Years Later
Words Without Borders (ed.)
(World)
The Wall in My Head
Xiao Hong (China)
Ma Bo'le's Second Life

CPSIA information can be obtained
at www.ICGtesting.com
Printed in the USA
JSHW010759110123
36043JS00001B/2

9 781948 830508